PRAISE FOR ALEX KAVA

"Alex Kava is a master. Her heroine, Special Agent Maggie O'Dell is one of the classic characters of the thriller genre."
— *Steve Berry, New York Times bestselling author*

"Kava's short scenes with cliffhanger endings are spot on." — *The Boston Globe*

"Maggie, who handles forensic evidence with ease can give Patricia Cornwell's Kay Scarpetta a run for her money." — *Booklist*

"O'Dell could be Reacher's long-lost twin."
— *Lee Child, New York Times bestselling author*

"Twisted plots, shocking characters, breakneck pacing. Guaranteed to keep you up all night."
— *Lisa Gardner, New York Times bestselling author*

"Tension, suspense, masterful twists-Alex Kava's writing has it all. This is a fantastic thriller."
— *Crimespace*

"A pro, Kava writes as coolly and adroitly as O'Dell profiles. Supremely paced."
— *The Lincoln Journal Star*

"Rip-roaring action that only builds in intensity with every page."
— *Tess Gerritsen, New York Times bestselling author*

ALEX KAVA

OFF THE GRID

Prairie Wind Publishing
18149 Trailridge Road
Omaha, Nebraska 68135
www.pwindpub.com

Publisher's Note: This is a work of fiction. Names, characters, places, and incidents are a product of the author's imagination. Locales and public names are sometimes used for atmospheric purposes. Any resemblance to actual people, living or dead, or to businesses, companies, events, institutions, or locales is completely coincidental.

Interior design & formatting: Deb Carlin, Prairie Wind Publishing
Book cover design: Deb Carlin, Prairie Wind Publishing

Ordering Information:
Quantity sales. Special discounts are available on quantity purchases by corporations, associations, and others. For details, contact Deb Carlin at the address above.

Off The Grid / Alex Kava. -- 1st edition
ISBN: 978-0-9836761-9-5

Printed in the United States of America
10 9 8 7 6 5 4 3 2

ALSO BY ALEX KAVA

OFF THE GRID

A collection of short stories
and one novella featuring
Maggie O'Dell.

TABLE OF CONTENTS

INTRODUCTION BY ALEX KAVA

Over the years I've written several short stories and a couple of novellas. All have been published either in anthologies or as larger ebooks. All but one of these short works includes FBI profiler, Special Agent Maggie O'Dell. And although you may have read one or two of them, I'm very excited to finally offer them as a collection for the first time.

When Deb Carlin started putting this collection together I realized that not only do these Maggie short works have a chronology, but all of them can be read as companion pieces to my Maggie novels. For example: *A Breath of Hot Air* takes place the first night that Maggie arrives in Pensacola, Florida, after spending the day with the Coast Guard flight crew of *Damaged*. The novella *Electric Blue* sets the stage and provides background for the novel, *Breaking Creed*. And in the novella, *Cold Metal Night* I purposely bring Nick Morrelli and Maggie back together one more time for readers who love Nick.

So for those of you who have read my novels as well as those new readers who are picking up this collection and reading my work for the first time, I thought it might be fun for you to know where these short works fit in with my novels. Of course they can be read and enjoyed individually.

Here's the list of the Maggie O'Dell novels with the short works inserted where they were meant to be:

A Perfect Evil
Split Second
The Soul Catcher
Goodnight, Sweet Mother (short story)
At the Stroke of Madness
A Necessary Evil
Exposed
Black Friday
A Breath of Hot Air (short story)
Damaged
Hotwire
Cold Metal Night (novella)
Fireproof
Stranded
Electric Blue (novella)
Breaking Creed
Silent Creed
Before Evil (2017)
Lost Creed (2018)
Desperate Creed (2019)
Hidden Creed (2020)

I hope you enjoy this collection. If you are not already a member of my VIR (Very Important Reader) Club, I invite you to join. We never share your information and you get to hear about giveaways and my book tour events as well as be included on my annual Christmas card list. To sign up and for more information about my books, go to www.alexkava.com. And I love to chat with my readers on Facebook at https://www.facebook.com/alexkava.books/

For the record here's where these short works have appeared previously:

Goodnight, Sweet Mother, "THRILLER: Stories to Keep You Up All Night," anthology edited by James Patterson, 2006.

A Breath of Hot Air, co-written with Patricia A. Bremmer, "Florida Heat Wave," anthology edited by Michael Lister, 2010.

After Dark, co-written with Deb Carlin, "First Thrills," anthology edited by Lee Child, 2010.

Cold Metal Night is one of three novellas that make up "Slices of Night," which also includes novellas by J.T. Ellison and Erica Spindler, 2010.

Electric Blue is one of three novellas that make up "Storm Season," which also includes novellas by J.T. Ellison and Erica Spindler, 2011.

OFF THE GRID

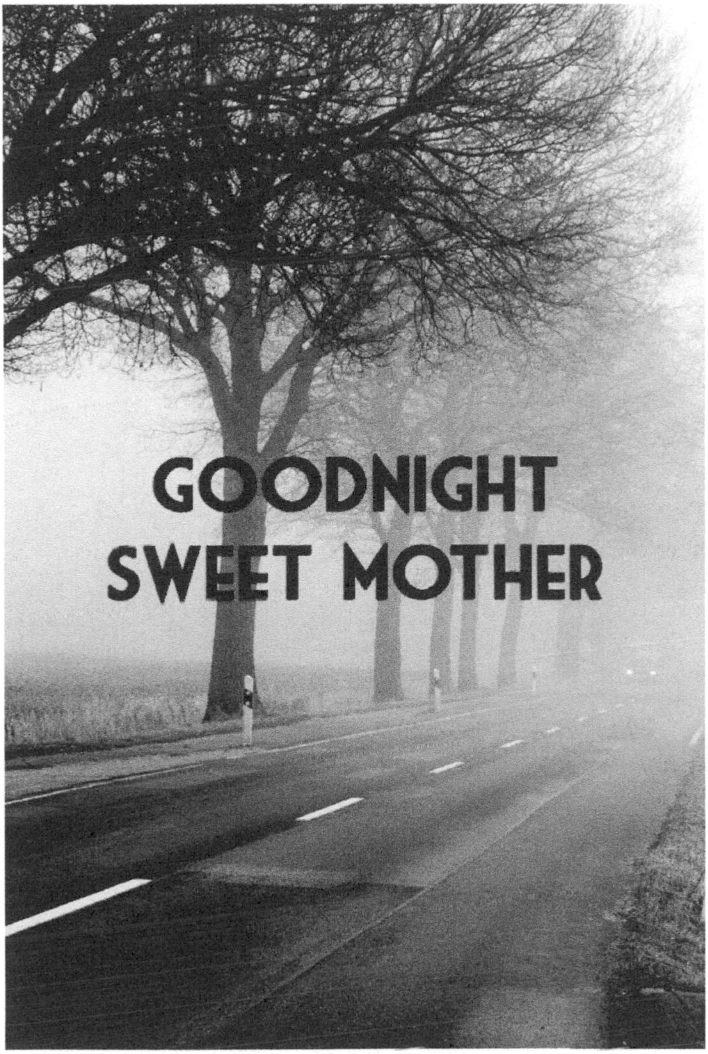
GOODNIGHT
SWEET MOTHER

GOODNIGHT SWEET MOTHER

Virginia

MAGGIE O'DELL KNEW this road trip with her mother was a mistake long before she heard the sickening scrape of metal grinding against metal, before she smelled the burning rubber of skidding tires.

Hours earlier she had declared it a mistake even as she slid into a cracked red vinyl booth in a place called Freddie's Dine -- actually Diner if you counted the faded area where an "r" had once been. The diner wasn't a part of the mistake. It didn't bother her eating in places that couldn't afford to replace an "r". After all, she had gobbled cheeseburgers in autopsy suites and had enjoyed deli sandwiches in an abandoned rock quarry while surrounded by barrels stuffed with dead bodies. No, the little diner could actually be called quaint.

It was not the problem.

Maggie had stared at a piece of apple pie ala mode the waitress named Rita had plopped down in front her before splashing more coffee into hers and her mother's cups. Nevermind the fact that she didn't drink coffee. For some reason she was willing to forgive her mother that mistake. But, the pie – *how could she forget that?*

The slice had looked perfectly fine and even smelled freshly baked, served warm so that the ice cream had begun to melt and trickle off the edges. The pie, itself, wasn't really the problem either, although without much effort Maggie had easily envisioned blood instead of ice cream dripping down onto the white bone china plate. She hated that just the scent of it had made her nauseated. She had to take a sip of water, close her eyes and steady herself before opening her eyes again to see ice cream instead of blood.

No, the real problem had been that Maggie didn't order the pie. Her mother had. Along with the coffee.

And that small gesture forced Maggie, once again, to wonder if Kathleen O'Dell was simply insensitive or if she honestly did not remember. How could she not remember the incident that could trigger her daughter's sudden uncontrollable nausea? How could she not remember one of the few times Maggie had shared something, anything from her life as an FBI profiler?

Of course, that incident had been several years ago and back then her mother had been drinking

Jack Daniels in tumblers instead of shot glasses, goading Maggie into arresting her if she didn't like it. Maggie remembered all too vividly what she had told her mother. She told her she didn't waste time arresting suicidal alcoholics. She should have stopped there, but didn't. Instead, she ended up pulling out and tossing onto her mother's glass-top coffee table Poloraids from the crime scene she had just left.

"This is what I do for a living," she had told her mother as if the woman needed a shocking reminder.

And Maggie remembered purposely dropping the last most brilliant one on top of the pile, the photo a close-up of a container left on the victim's kitchen counter. Maggie would never forget that plastic take-out container, nor its contents – a perfect piece of apple pie with the victim's bloody spleen neatly arranged on top.

That her mother had chosen to forget or block it out shouldn't surprise Maggie. The one survival tactic the woman possessed was her strong sense of denial, her ability to pretend certain incidents had simply not happened. How else could she explain letting her twelve-year-old daughter fend for herself while she stumbled home drunk each night, bringing along the stranger who had supplied her for that particular night?

It wasn't until one of Kathleen O'Dell's gentleman friends suggested a threesome with mother, daughter and himself that it occurred to her mother to get a hotel room. Maggie had had to learn at an early age to take care of herself. She had grown up alone, and only now, years after her divorce, did she realize she associated being alone with being safe from anyone who could hurt her.

But her mother had come a long way since then, or so Maggie had believed. That was before this road trip, before she had ordered the piece of apple pie. Perhaps Maggie should see it for what it was – the perfect microcosm of their relationship, a relationship that should never include road trips or the mere opportunity for sharing a piece of pie at a quaint, little diner.

She had watched as her mother sipped coffee in-between swiping up bites of her own pie. As an FBI criminal profiler Maggie O'Dell tracked killers for a living and yet a simple outing with her mother could conjure up images of a serial killer's leftover surprises tucked away in take-out containers.

Just another day at the office.

She supposed she wasn't as good as her mother at denial, but that wasn't necessarily a bad thing.

Suddenly Kathleen O'Dell had pointed her fork at something over Maggie's shoulder, unable to speak because, of course, it was impolite to talk with a full mouth, never mind that during her brief and rare lapses into motherhood she constantly preached it was also impolite to point. Maggie didn't budge, ignoring her, which was also silly if she thought it would in any way punish her mother for her earlier insensitivity. Besides it had only resulted in a more significant poke at the air from her mother's fork.

"That guy's a total ass," she was finally able to whisper.

Maggie hadn't been able to resist. She stole a glance, needing to see the *"total ass"* she was about to defend, because that was usually what her immediate reaction was, to come to the defense of anyone her mother would dare to condemn on sight only.

He had seemed too ordinary to need Maggie's defense. Ever the profiler she had found herself immediately assessing him. She saw a tall, thin middle-aged man with a receding hairline, weak chin and wire-rimmed glasses. He wore a white oxford shirt, a size too large and sagging even though he had tried to tuck it neatly into the waistband of wrinkled trousers – trousers which were belted below the beginning paunch of a man who spent too much time behind a desk.

He had slid into one of the corner booths and grabbed one of the laminated menus from behind the table's condiment holder. Immediately he had the menu unfolded in front of him, hunched over it and was searching for his selection while he pulled silverware from the bundled napkin.

Again, all very ordinary. An ordinary guy taking a break from work to get a bite to eat. But then Maggie had seen the old woman, shuffling to the table, holding onto the backs of the other booths along the way, her cane not enough to steady her. That's when Maggie realized her mother's pronouncement had little to do with the man's appearance and everything to do with the fact that he had left this poor woman to shuffle and fumble her way to their table.

He hadn't even looked up at the her as she struggled to lower herself in-between the table and the bench, dropping her small, fragile frame onto the seat and then scooting inch by inch across the vinyl while her cane thump-thumped its way in behind her.

Maggie had turned away, not wanting to watch any longer. She hated to agree with her mother. She hated even more the "tsk, tsk" sound her mother had made, loud enough for others at the diner to hear, perhaps even the total ass.

Funny how things worked. Now miles away from the diner and back on the road, Maggie would give anything to hear that "tsk, tsk" rather than her mother's high-pitched scream.

In fact, had she not been distracted by her mother's screams she may have noticed the blur of black steel sliding alongside her car much sooner. Certainly she would have noticed before the monster pickup rammed into her Toyota Corolla a second time, shoving her off the side of the road, all the while ripping and tearing metal.

Was that her front bumper dragging from the pickup's grill?

It looked as though the hulking truck had taken a bite out of her poor car.

What the hell was this guy doing?

"I can't believe you didn't see him," her mother scolded, the previous screams leaving her usual raspy voice high-pitched and almost comical. "Where the hell did he come from?" she added, already contradicting her first comment.

She strained against her seat belt, reaching and grabbing for the Skittles candies she had been eating, now scattered across the seat and plopping to the floor mats like precious rainbow beads from a broken necklace.

"I didn't see him," Maggie confessed, gaining control of her car and bringing it to a stop on the dirt shoulder of the two-lane highway.

God! Her hands were shaking.

She gripped the steering wheel harder to make them stop. When that didn't work she dropped them into her lap. She felt sweat trickle down her back.

How could she not have seen him?

The pickup had pulled off the road more than five car lengths ahead, the taillights winking at them through a cloud of dust. In-between lie the Toyota's mangled front bumper, twisted and discarded like roadside debris.

"Don't go telling him that," her mother whispered.

"Excuse me?"

"Don't go admitting to him that you didn't see him. You don't want your car insurance skyrocketing."

"Are you suggesting I lie?"

"I'm suggesting you keep your mouth shut."

"I'm a federal law officer."

"No, you said you left your badge and gun at home. Today you're a plain ole citizen, minding your own business."

Kathleen O'Dell popped several of the Skittles into her mouth, and Maggie couldn't help thinking how much the bright colored candy reminded her of the nerve pills her mother used to take, often times washing them down with vodka or Scotch. How could she eat at a time like this, especially when it had been less than an hour since they had left the diner? But Maggie knew she should be grateful for the recent exchange of addictions.

"I haven't been in a car accident since college," Maggie said, rifling through her wallet for proof of insurance and driver's license.

"Whatever you do don't ask for the cops to be called," she whispered again, leaning toward Maggie as though they were co-conspirators.

She and her mother had never been on the same side of any issue. Suddenly a black pickup rams into the side of their car and they're instant friends. Okay, maybe not friends. Co-conspirators did seem more appropriate.

"He side-swiped me," Maggie defended herself anyway despite her mother being on her side.

"Doesn't matter. Calling the cops only makes it worse."

Maggie glanced at her mother who was still popping the candies like they were antacids. People often remarked on their resemblance to each other – the auburn hair, fair complexion and dark brown eyes. And yet, much of the time they spent together Maggie felt like a stranger to this woman who couldn't even remember why apple pie – or any pie, for that matter – made her nauseated.

"I am 'the cops,'" Maggie said, impatient that this too was something she constantly needed to remind her mother.

"No, you're not, Sweetie. FBI's not the same thing. Oh, Jesus. It's him. That ass from the diner."

He had gotten out of the pickup but was surveying the damage on his own vehicle.

"Just go," her mother said, grabbing Maggie's arm and giving it a shove to start the car.

"Leave the scene of an accident?"

"It was his fault anyway. He's not going to report you."

"Too late," Maggie said, catching in her rearview mirror the flashing lights of a state trooper pulling off the road and coming up behind her. Her mother noticed the glance and twisted around in her seat.

"Son of a bitch!"

"Mom!" For all her faults, Kathleen O'Dell rarely swore.

"This has not been a good trip."

Maggie stared at her, dumbfounded that her mother might also think the trip had been as miserable an outing for her as it had been for Maggie.

"Promise me you won't play hero," Kathleen O'Dell grabbed at Maggie's arm again. "Don't go telling them you're a federal officer."

"He'll actually be easier on us," Maggie told her. "There's a bond between law enforcement officers."

To this her mother let out a hysterical laugh. "Oh Sweetie, if you really think a state trooper will appreciate advice or help from the feds, and a woman at that..."

God, she hated to agree with her mother for a second time in the same day. But she was right. Maggie had experienced it almost every time she went into a rural community. Small town cops tended to be defensive and intimidated by her. Sometimes state troopers fit into that category, too.

She opened her car door and felt her mother still tugging at her arm.

"Promise me," Kathleen O'Dell said in a tone that reminded Maggie of when she was a little girl. Her mother would insist Maggie promise not to tell one of a variety of indiscretions her mother would have committed that week.

"You don't have to worry," Maggie said, pulling her arm away and escaping the car, escaping her mother's hold.

"My, my, what a mess," the state trooper called out, his hands on his belt buckle as he approached.

He glanced at Maggie's car then continued to the bumper where he came to a stop. He looked from one vehicle to another then back, shaking his head, his mirrored sunglasses giving Maggie a view of the wreckage in reverse of what he saw.

He was young. Even without seeing his eyes she could tell. A bit short, though she didn't think the Virginia State Police had a height requirement any longer, but he was in good shape and he knew it. Maggie realized his hands on his belt buckle wasn't in case he needed to get at his weapon quickly but rather to emphasize his flat stomach, probably perfect six-pack abs under the gray, neatly tucked shirt.

"Let me guess," he said, addressing Maggie as he watched the owner of the pickup stomping around his vehicle. "You lost control. Maybe touching up your makeup."

"Excuse me?" Maggie was sure she must have heard him wrong.

"Cell phone, maybe?" He grinned at her. "It's okay. I know you ladies love to talk and drive at the same time."

"This wasn't my fault." She wanted to get her badge from the glove compartment.

She glanced back just in time to see her mother shoot her a cautionary look and she knew exactly what she was saying with her eyes, "See it's always worse when the cops get involved."

"Sure, it wasn't your fault," he said, not even attempting to disguise his sarcasm.

"He was the one driving erratically." Maggie knew it sounded lame as soon as it left her mouth. The boy trooper had already accomplished what he had set out to do – he had succeeded in making her defensive.

"Hey, sir," he called out to the pickup owner who finally came over and joined them, standing over Maggie's mangled bumper, looking at it like he had no idea how it had gotten there. "Sir, were you driving erratically?"

"Oh for God's sake," Maggie said then held her breath before she said anything more.

She wanted to hit this cocky son of a bitch, and it had been a long time since she had wanted to hit somebody she didn't know.

"I was trying to pass and she shoved right into me."

"That's a lie," Maggie's mother yelled over the top of the car. Both men stared at her as though only now realizing she was there.

"Oh good," the boy trooper said, "We have a witness."

"My mom's in the pickup," the guy said, pointing a thumb back behind him.

They all turned to see a skinny, white leg sticking out from the passenger door. But that was as far as the old woman had gotten. Her cane hung on the inside door handle. Her foot, encased in what looked like a thin bedroom slipper, dangled about eight inches from the running board of the pickup.

"Well, I guess I'll have to just take a look and see what happened. See whose story's most *accurate*," he said with yet another grin.

Maggie couldn't help wondering where he had trained. No academy she knew of taught that smug, arrogant grin. Someone must have told him it gave him an edge, disarmed his potential opponents. After all, it was tough to argue with someone who already had his mind made up and was willing to humiliate you if you didn't agree. It was a tactic of a much older, mature lawman, one who could afford to be cocky because he knew more than he ever cared to know about human nature. One who could back up that attitude if challenged or threatened. This boy trooper, in Maggie's opinion, wasn't deserving of such a tactic.

As soon as she was close enough to see his badge and read his nametag she decided she knew a few tactics of her own. One stripe to his patch meant he was a trooper first class. He hadn't made corporal or sergeant yet.

"The skid marks should tell an accurate enough story, Sergeant Blake," Maggie said, getting his attention. Then she let him see her eyes glance at the insignia and added, "Sorry, I guess it's Trooper Blake."

The grin slid off his face. It was one thing to notice his name, quite another to address him by his rank. Most people didn't have a clue whether state troopers were officers or deputies, sergeants or troopers.

"Sure, sure. That's possible," he nodded. "I need to see both your driver's licenses before I check out skid marks." And he put his hand out.

Maggie resisted the urge to smile at what seemed a transparent attempt to gain control, to keep his edge. No problem. She already had hers ready and handed it to him. The pickup driver started digging in his shirt pocket then twisted and patted at his back pants pockets when suddenly there came a screech – something between a wail and a holler.

It came from inside his vehicle, "Harold? *Harrrrrold?*"

All of them stopped and turned, but nothing more had immerged from the pickup. Nothing besides the white leg still dangling. Then Maggie, her mother and Trooper Blake all stared at Harold, watching as a crimson tide washed up his neck, coloring his entire face. His ears were such a brilliant red Maggie wondered if they actually hurt or burned. But just as he had paid her no attention in the diner, Harold made no attempt to acknowledge the old woman now. Instead, he pulled out a thick, bulging wad of leather that was his wallet and began to rummage through it.

While Trooper Blake took their drivers licenses and headed back to his patrol car, Harold surveyed the damage to his pickup once more. He shook his head while making that annoying "tsk, tsk" sound that Maggie's mother had used earlier. He still hadn't checked on his mother. Instead, Harold stomped up to the highway. Evidently he wanted to see what evidence had been marked in rubber.

Maggie stayed in her own territory, wanting to tell Harold that he should be grateful. His damage was minimal compared to her ripped-off bumper and smashed driver's side. The gaping wound in her car's front end now had protruding pieces of metal shards like daggers. What a mess! There was no way she was taking blame for any of this.

She hadn't been paying much attention to her mother and certainly not keeping track of her whereabouts. It had been several minutes before Maggie noticed Kathleen O'Dell now standing in front of the opened passenger door of the pickup. Her hands were on her hips. She was tilting her head and nodding as if concentrating on what the old woman inside the vehicle had to say. Just then her mother looked back, caught Maggie's eyes and waved her over.

Maggie's first thought was that the poor woman was injured. Harold hadn't even bothered to check on her. Why hadn't she thought of it sooner? She rushed to her mother's side, glancing over her shoulder but both men were focused elsewhere.

The two women were whispering to each other. From what Maggie could see of the old woman she didn't look like she was in pain. However, there were several old bruises on her arms – old because they were already turning a greenish yellow.

The woman's arthritic fingers tapped the seat with an uncontrollable tremor. Maggie remembered how slow and vulnerable Harold's mother had looked back at the diner. She seemed even smaller and more fragile here inside the cab of the pickup with her spine curling her into a constant hunched over position.

"He does scare me sometimes," the woman said to Kathleen O'Dell although her eyes were looking over Maggie.

"It's not right," Maggie's mother told the woman. Then realizing Maggie was by her side she turned to Maggie. "Wanda says he hits her sometimes." She pointed to the woman's bruises and Wanda folded her thin arms as if to hide the evidence.

"The accident was his fault, Kathleen. He ran right into the side of your car. But you know I can't say that." She rubbed her shoulders as if they, too, were sore and bruised underneath her cotton blouse.

Maggie watched the two women, surprised that they spoke to each other as if they were old friends. Why was it that Kathleen O'Dell could so easily befriend a stranger but not have a clue about her own daughter?

"Wanda says that sometimes he comes after her with a hammer at night," she whispered while she glanced around. Feeling safe, she continued, "He tells her she might not wake up in the morning."

"He's a wicked boy, my Harold," the old woman said, shaking her head, her fingers drumming faster now as if out of her control.

"What's going on?" Harold yelled, hurrying back from his examination of the skid marks.

Maggie watched the old woman tense up at the sound of his voice.

"We're just chatting with your mom," Maggie told him. "That's not a problem, is it?"

"Not unless she's telling you lies," he said a bit out of breath. "She lies all the time."

Maggie thought it seemed a strange thing to say about your mother, but Harold said it as casually as if it were part of an introduction, just another one of his mother's quaint personality traits. He didn't, however, look as casual when he noticed Trooper Blake approaching them.

"Funny, she was just saying the same about you," Kathleen O'Dell said.

Maggie wanted to catch her mother's attention long enough to shoot her a warning look. No such luck.

"What's going on?" This time it was Trooper Blake's question.

"She says you beat her," Kathleen O'Dell didn't hold back.

"Kathleen, you promised," Wanda wailed at her.

Maggie grabbed her mother's arm and tried to lead her away, but she pulled free and continued. "She said you come after her with a hammer."

There was no grin on Trooper Blake's face now, and Harold's resumed a softer crimson color than the earlier shade.

"For God's sake," he muttered with an attempted laugh. "She says that about everybody. The old lady's crazy."

"Really?" Trooper Blake asked and Maggie noticed his hands on his belt were a bit closer to his weapon.

"Two days ago she said the same thing about her mailman." Harold wiped at the sweat on his forehead. "For God's sake, she lies about every-thing."

Maggie looked back at Wanda who had pulled herself deeper inside the pickup, and now she had her cane in her shaking hands as if worried she might need a weapon of her own.

Maggie wasn't sure what happened next. It all seemed like a blur even to a trained law officer like herself. Too often that was the way things happened. Words were exchanged. Tempers flair and suddenly there's no taking back any of it.

Trooper Blake said something about taking Harold in to answer some questions. To which Harold said he had had enough of "this nonsense." He started to walk away, going around to the driver's side of the pickup as if to simply leave.

Maybe a more experienced state trooper would have been more commanding with his voice or his presence. Trooper Blake felt it necessary to empha-size his order by reaching out and clamping down on Harold's arm. Harold shoved at the trooper. Blake grabbed at him again and the two men fought.

Before Maggie could interfere Harold broke free but stumbled backward. As he fell to the ground, the back of his head cracked against the ripped met-al of his own pickup. The sound made her wince – a sickening thump.

Harold's eyes were wide open, but that blank stare told her he was dead even before she bent over to take his pulse.

THREE HOURS LATER Maggie and her mother took Wanda home. Maggie tried to follow the woman's directions despite them changing several times in route. For a few minutes it felt as if they were going around in circles. But Maggie recognized the woman was in shock, and she patiently waited for her to issue a new set of directions each time.

Other than getting a bit mixed up, Wanda hadn't said much. Back at the state police station, Kathleen O'Dell had asked if there was someone they should call. Even after Maggie decided to drive the old woman home, Kathleen still kept asking if there was anyone who could come stay with her. But Wanda only shook her head.

Finally they pulled up to the curb of a quaint, yellow bungalow at the end of a street lined with huge pine trees and large green lawns.

"We'll help you to the door," Maggie said and she started unbuckling her seatbelt and reaching for the door handle.

"No, no. I'll be fine. You've already done enough." And she opened her car door. As she began climbing out she stopped and all of a sudden Wanda said, "I don't know what I'll do without that boy. He was all I had."

For the first time, she sounded sad.

There was silence. Maggie and her mother looked at each other. Was it simply the shock? Survivor's guilt?

"But you said he beat you?" Kathleen O'Dell reminded her.

"Oh, no, *no*. Harold would never lay a hand on me."

"You said he came after you at night with a hammer."

This time both Maggie and her mother turned to stare over the seat as if emphasizing their confusion.

"My Harold would never hurt me," Wanda said quite confidently as she eased herself out of the car. "It's that wicked Mr. Sumpter, who brings the mail. I know he has a hammer in that mailbag," she said without hesitation.

Then she slammed the car door behind her and without another word, she started waddling up the sidewalk.

Maggie and her mother stared at each other, both paralyzed and speechless. It wasn't until Harold's mother was climbing up the yellow house's front porch that Maggie noticed the woman no longer struggled. She was walking just fine despite leaving her cane in the back seat of Maggie's vehicle.

AUTHOR'S NOTE: *Goodnight, Sweet Mother* was first published in 2006 in the anthology, *Thriller: Stories to Keep You Up All Night*, edited by James Patterson along with 29 other original short stories written by some of the best thriller writers in the business.

A BREATH OF
HOT AIR

A BREATH OF HOT AIR

Pensacola Beach, Florida

THE POUNDING came from somewhere outside her nightmare. Maggie O'Dell fought her way to consciousness. Her breathing came in gulps as if she had been running. In her nightmare she had been. But now she sat up in bed and strained to hear over the drumming of her heartbeat as she tried to recognize the moonlit room that surrounded her.

It was the breeze coming through the patio door that jumpstarted her memory. Hot, moist air tickled free the damp hair on her forehead. She could practically taste the salt of the Gulf waters just outside her room.

The Hilton Hotel on Pensacola Beach, she remembered.

A digital clock beside her with glow-in-the-dark numbers clicked and flipped to 12:47. She was here on assignment, despite a category 5 hurricane barreling toward the Florida Panhandle. But forty minutes earlier all had been calm. Not a cloud in sight to block the full moon. Only the waves predicted the coming storm, already rising higher with white caps breaking and crashing against the shore. Maggie liked the sound and had left the patio door open – but only a sliver – keeping the security bar engaged. She had hoped the sound would lull her to sleep. It must have worked, at least for forty minutes. That's if you considered nightmares with fishing coolers stuffed full of body parts anything close to sleep.

She hadn't been able to shut off the adrenaline from her afternoon adventure, hovering two hundred feet above the Gulf of Mexico in a Coast Guard helicopter. It hadn't been the strangest crime scene Maggie had ever visited in her ten years with the FBI. The aircrew had recovered a marine cooler floating in the waters just off Pensacola Beach. But instead of finding some fisherman's discarded catch of the day, the crew was shocked to discover human body parts – a torso, three hands and a foot – all carefully wrapped in thick plastic.

However, it hadn't been the body parts that had tripped Maggie into what she called her "nightmare cycle," a vicious loop of snapshots from her memory's scrapbook. Some people slipped into REM cycle, Maggie had her nightmare cycle. No, it wasn't the severed body parts. She had seen and dealt with her share of those. It was the helicopter flight and dangling two hundred feet above control. That's really why she had opened the patio doors earlier. She desperately wanted to replace the thundering sound of the rotors.

The pounding started again and she jerked up, only now remembering what had wakened her.

Someone was at the door.

"Ms. O'Dell." A man's voice. High pitched. No one she recognized.

Maggie stumbled out of bed, pulled on khaki shorts and a T-shirt over damp, sticky skin. She had shut off the room's A/C when she opened the patio door and the air inside was now as hot and humid as it was outside. Florida in August. What was she thinking shutting off the A/C?

She picked up her holstered revolver on the way to the door. Her fingers slid around the handle, her index finger settling on the trigger, but she kept the gun in its holster.

"Yes, who is it?" She asked, standing back and to the side of the door as she waved her other hand in front of the peephole. An old habit, borne of paranoia and self-preservation. If there were a shooter on the other side, he'd be waiting for his target to press an eye against the peephole.

"The night manager. Robert. I mean Robert Evans." The voice sounded young and panicked. "We have a situation. My boss said you're with the FBI. I'm sorry to wake you. It's sort of an emergency."

This time Maggie glanced out the peephole. The fisheye version made Robert Evans look geekier than he probably was – tall and lanky with nervous energy that kept him rocking from one foot to the other. He tugged at his shirt collar, one finger planted inside as though it was the only thing keeping his company-issued tie from strangling him.

"What kind of an emergency?"

She watched his bobble-size head jerk left then right, making sure no one else was in the hallway. Then he leaned closer to the door and tried to keep his voice low but the panic kicked it into a whispered screech.

"I think I got a dead guy in Room 347."

Hilton Hotel Tiki Bar

GLEN KARST SIPPED his bourbon from a corner stool at the outdoor tiki bar. To his left he had a perfect view of the hotel's back door and to his right was a sight that looked like it was taken off a postcard – silver-topped waves shimmering in the moonlight, lapping at sugar-white sands. If he ever decided to afford himself a vacation this would be a great place, that is, if he didn't mind sweating. After midnight and it felt like he had a hot, damp towel draped around his neck that he couldn't knock off.

Didn't help that he was exhausted. It had taken him most of the day to get here. All flights to Pensacola had been canceled because of Hurricane Isaac, which meant the closest Glen could get from Denver, was Atlanta. He'd spent the last six hours in a rent-a-car, a compact, the only thing left on such short notice. Not quite his style, nor his body's.

But he couldn't blame the Ford Escort for all the tension in the small of his back. A good deal of it had been there before he began this journey, one that he hoped wouldn't be a wild goose chase. As a veteran detective Glen Karst had come to rely on his hunches, his gut instinct, as much as he did his expertise. But coming this far on such short notice and with a hurricane coming, he figured he had maybe twenty-four hours.

A flash of light came from behind him and Glen glanced over his shoulder. A group of college kids mugged for a camera, all holding up bright red drinks in a toast.

Hurricane glasses, Glen noticed, shook his head and smiled.

Sure didn't look like a hurricane was anywhere near. The beach's restaurants and bars were full of tourists and residents, some spilling out onto the shore and into the parking lots. He'd also noticed quite a few pickups and moving vans packed and stacked full of belongings, ready to roll.

It was Florida. Glen figured the residents knew the drill. They'd been through it enough times in the last several years. But if they were still out eating and drinking then he knew he still had time.

He pulled a brochure from his shirt pocket, laid it on the bar next to his glass and smoothed out the crease. The man in the photo had added a good thirty pounds to his hefty frame. His blond hair had been cut short, dyed dark brown and peppered with gray at the temples. The goatee was new and attempted to hide the beginning of a double chin. At a glimpse, the man looked nothing like Dr. Thomas Gruber, but Glen recognized the eyes, deep-set and ice blue. In his arrogance the good doctor had failed to disguise the one trait that betrayed him most.

"They canceled," said a young man three bar stools over, pointing at Glen's brochure.

"What's that?"

"The conference. It's been canceled because of the hurricane."

"Damn, are you sure?"

"Don't take this the wrong way, but you don't look like a doctor."

"That's good, cause I don't like doctors."

The guy stood up, his drink in one hand and nodded at the stool next to Glen, "You mind?"

"I'm not expecting anyone."

Glen sipped his bourbon, not giving the guy much attention. But in the time it took for the man to sidle up next to him, Glen had noted the man's short cropped hair – military – would have been Glen's first guess except for the Rolex, Sperry deck shoes and Ralph Lauren polo that he left untucked over khaki cargo shorts. Expensive wares for a guy, who according to Glen's estimate, was probably thirty at the most.

"Name's Joe Black," he tipped his glass at Glen instead of offering his hand. The glass was a rocks glass like his own. Scotch or bourbon, neat.

"Glen." From the corner of his eyes he could see Joe Black assessing him, too. He was cool, calm, and took only a casual glimpse at the brochure on the bar between them. "So you go to these conferences?"

"You might say I'm a regular."

Glen gave him a sidelong look. "Hell, you don't look like a doctor either."

Joe laughed, but he didn't bother to answer, nor did he look like he was going to. However, his eyes darted to the brochure again before he shifted on the bar stool and reached for his glass.

"You know this doctor?" Glen tapped the photo looking down at it, pretending he needed to look in order to remember the name, "This Dr. Eric Foster?"

But in fact, he had memorized every detail about Dr. Foster alias Dr. Gruber. The only thing he couldn't figure out is why Gruber would risk coming back to the states.

Just over a year ago Gruber had fled Colorado after being the main suspect in a triple homicide. Gruber had abandoned his surgical practice, skipped out on a million dollar mortgage and left his wife penniless. He had escaped to South America. Somewhere in Brazil, according to Glen's last effort in tracking him. Rumor was that the good doctor might be trafficking body parts, even going as far as buying kidneys from poor struggling schmucks who had nothing else to sell.

Ironically, the conference that had Gruber scheduled as a featured speaker bragged about having human specimens for surgeons to perfect their skills. Nothing illegal. Glen had checked it out. These conferences took place all over the country though usually at some beachfront resort as an added incentive. Medical device companies planned and arranged them, offering surgeons all-expense paid trips in exchange for them to come try out the company's newest gadgets and hopefully put in several orders before they returned home.

The fact was the triple homicide in Colorado remained open. No other suspects. All evidence pointed to Gruber and the bastard had slipped away during the investigation. Glen was more than anxious to finally nail the guy.

"Yeah, I know Foster. You might say he's my competition," Joe Black finally said without offering anything more. He waved down the bartender and pointed to his glass. "Another Johnnie Walker,

Black Label." Then to Glen he said, "How bout you? Another Buffalo Trace?"

Glen hid his surprise. He simply nodded at the bartender. Joe Black knew what he was drinking. Why the hell had this guy been watching him?

"So what do you want with Dr. Foster?" Joe asked.

"Just want to have a friendly chat."

"You a cop?"

"I don't look like a doctor, but I look like a cop, huh?"

Joe shrugged and went quiet while the bartender placed fresh drinks in front of them.

"If not a cop, maybe a jealous husband?" This time he looked at Glen, waiting to see his reaction.

Glen fidgeted with his glass but didn't say a word. Sometimes people filled in the silence if you waited long enough.

It seemed to work.

Satisfied with Glen's response – or rather his non-response – Joe continued, "I told him it'd catch up with him one of these days. So the blond with all the expensive jewelry? She must be yours?"

This was easier than Glen expected. "Is she with him now?"

Joe nodded and tipped back the rest of his Scotch. "Finish your drink," he told Glen. "I'll take you up to his room."

Glen could hardly believe it. He looked the guy over, this time allowing his suspicions to show. "Why would you do me any favors?"

"Maybe because I don't much like the bastard myself."

AS SOON AS MAGGIE walked into the room she knew that the big man sprawled on his back in the king-size bed had not died of natural causes. His bloodshot eyes stared at the ceiling. His mouth twisted into a sardonic grin. Trousers lay crumpled in a pile on the floor, a belt half pulled from the loops. Shoes peeked out from under.

"Who found him?" Maggie glanced back at Evans.

The night manager had grown pale before they reached the room. Now he stayed in the open doorway, unwilling to move any farther into the room.

"Someone from housekeeping. There was a request for more towels."

Evans couldn't see the body from his post inside the doorwell and Maggie realized he couldn't see her either. Without stepping on or touching anything, she ventured closer. The dead man wore bright blue boxers and a button-down shirt, half unbuttoned. His skin looked like it was on fire – bright red, but not from sunburn.

"He probably had a heart attack, right?" Evans sounded hopeful.

"Was he alone?" Maggie asked, noticing an empty wine bottle with one glass on the nightstand.

"No one else is listed under his registration."

"But he wasn't alone," another voice said from outside in the hallway.

Maggie came around the bed, back into the entrance just in time to see two men standing over the night manager's bony shoulder.

"Are you from the sheriff's department?" she asked.

"I didn't call the sheriff's department," Evans said, bracing his hand on the doorway and making a barrier with his skinny arm.

"911?" Maggie tried again.

"I didn't call anyone," Evans said. Then with wide eyes and an attempted whisper, he leaned toward her and added, "My boss said to get you. *Only you.*"

"I'm Detective Glen Karst," the man in the hallway poked his arm over Evans, offering a badge and ID.

Maggie reached out and took the ID but instead of turning on the light in the entrance for the men to see in, she leaned into the bathroom using its light.

"You're a long way from home, Detective Karst." She handed him back his ID and stood with hands on her hips, waiting for his explanation while Evans kept up his pathetic barrier.

"I have reason to believe the man inside is a suspect in a triple homicide. I just want to ask him a few questions. Mr. Black told me –" Karst stopped, turned then looked around the hallway as though he'd lost something or someone. The man who had accompanied him was gone.

Maggie glanced at her watch. It was late and she was exhausted. She'd been on the road for half the day and dangling over the Gulf in a helicopter for the other half. Her forty-minute nap had been invaded by nightmares. This dead guy wasn't even her jurisdiction.

"Mr. Evans, I think you should go call the sheriff's department." She put a gentle hand on his shoulder, waiting for him to drop his arm from the doorjamb.

"The sheriff's department?" He said it like it still hadn't even occurred to him to do so.

"Yes." She kept eye contact, hoping to transfer her calm and cool composure over to him. "Detective Karst and I will secure the room until someone from the sheriff's department gets here."

Both Maggie and Karst watched Evans leave, his lanky frame wobbled like a drunk attempting to walk on tiptoes. He missed the turn for the elevators, stopped and backtracked, giving them an embarrassed wave then straightened up like a sleepwalker suddenly coming awake. Maggie waited until she heard the ping of the elevator before she turned back to the room.

"Don't touch anything," she told Detective Karst as she gestured for him to follow her inside.

"Don't worry about me. I didn't catch your name."

"Maggie O'Dell."

"You're not local law enforcement."

It wasn't a question. He said it with such certainty Maggie stopped in the entrance and looked back at him. She wanted to ask how he knew then decided it wasn't important.

"FBI. I'm down here on another assignment. The night manager thought it would be more convenient to wake me up rather than call the sheriff."

"Son of a bitch, don't tell me Foster's dead?" Karst asked as he came into view of the bed.

"Do you recognize him?"

He didn't need to come any closer. "Yeah, I do. He goes by Eric Foster, but his real name is Thomas Gruber. What's your guess? Suicide?"

"No."

"You sound pretty sure of yourself."

This time she smiled at him. "I do this for a living, Detective Karst."

"I'm not questioning your qualifications, just asking how you reached that conclusion."

Maggie pointed at the dead man's eyes. "Petechial hemorrhages."

Karst leaned closer. "His neck doesn't show any signs of strangulation."

"The ruptures probably occurred during convulsions, maybe seizures. He strangled but from the inside out."

He raised an eyebrow at her, waiting for more.

"I recognize that twist of the mouth and the bright red skin, almost cherry red. I've only seen this sort of skin discoloration once before but it's something I'll never forget. The tissue can't get any oxygen. It happens quickly. Ten to fifteen minutes."

"You think he was poisoned?"

Maggie nodded, impressed. The detective from Colorado was sharp.

Karst noticed her look and it was his turn to smile. "I do this for a living, too."

Then he started looking at the bedding, careful not to touch but bending over and searching the pillows.

"Usually there's vomit," he said and started sniffing the linens, now leaning even closer over the dead man. Then Karst's body stiffened and he stood up straight. "Cyanide."

"Excuse me?"

"I can smell it," he said. "Like bitter almonds."

Maggie came up beside Karst and he stepped back while she bent over the dead man's face. Only forty to fifty percent of people could smell the after-effects of cyanide. It was a genetic ability. The scent was faint but she could smell it, too.

"I thought it might be something like that," she said. "Cyanide stops cells from using oxygen. He would have felt like he was suffocating – a shortness of breath followed by dizziness. Then comes the confusion and possible seizures, bursting the capillaries in the eyes. Last would be cardiac arrest. All in a matter of minutes."

"Potassium cyanide is a crystal compound." Karst looked around the room and pointed to the wine bottle. "May have slipped it into the wine. Where does someone get cyanide these days?"

Maggie had to stop and think, retrieve the information from her memory bank. The case she had worked on had happened too many years ago – six young men in a cabin in the woods had chosen to obey their leader and take cyanide capsules rather than be taken into custody. She'd lost a friend that day – a fellow FBI agent – so the memory didn't come easily.

"Potassium cyanide is still used in several industries. Certain kinds of photography," she finally said. "Some processing of plastics, electroplating and gold plating in jewelry making. If a person buys it on a regular basis for their business it usually doesn't draw any attention."

Now she wanted to dismantle the memory and started looking over the room again. She plucked a tissue from its container on the nightstand and gently pressed her covered fingertip against the dead man's jaw then his neck. "No rigor."

"So he's been dead less than twelve hours."

"Maybe less than six. Rigor sets in more quickly with cyanide poisoning. You said he wasn't alone?" She turned to see Karst had moved to the desk and was lifting open a folded wallet using the tip of a pen. "What makes you think that someone was with him?"

"Guy I met at the bar downstairs told me he saw Gruber leave with a blond."

"The guy who took off as soon as he saw your badge?"

He glanced up at Maggie. "Coincidence?"

"I don't believe in coincidences."

"Me either. I'll bet he gave me a bogus name. Hell, he probably lied about the blond, too."

Maggie used the tissue again as she tipped a wastebasket out from under the nightstand. The only thing inside was another tissue, this one crumpled with a blotted stain of bright pink lipstick. She gently lifted it by a corner, pulling it up high enough to show Karst.

"Unless there's something a little freaky about Dr. Foster, I think your friend might have been telling the truth about the blond."

"I'll be damned."

Maggie took a good look at the stain under the light then gently placed it back where she had found it. Later she'd point it out to the sheriff's investigator.

"What did he do?" she asked.

Karst folded his arms and stared at the dead man. "His nurse was two-timing him with a rich ex-patient. He murdered her then took out the ex-patient even killing the guy's wife. Gruber set their house on fire, hoping to hide all the evidence. He cleaned out his medical practice's bank account along with his personal ones and high-tailed it to South America before we could even question him. Left his business partner and his wife with a load of bills and no cash."

"So there might be a few others beside you, looking for him."

"Not to mention some new enemies. The guy from the bar mentioned something about Gruber being his competition."

Maggie watched Karst's face. He was still grinding out the case in his mind. She checked her watch again.

"I'd say you no longer have a case, Detective Karst."

There was knock at the door followed by, "Sheriff's department."

GLEN KARST FOUND himself back down at the hotel's tiki bar. This time he and Maggie shared one of the high-top tables. He'd asked to buy her a drink and was surprised when the tough, no nonsense FBI agent ordered a Diet Pepsi. He ordered another Buffalo Trace, glancing around to see if Joe Black was somewhere close by, watching again.

The waves had kicked up and the moon had slid over a bit. A breeze almost made the hot, humid air feel good. The beach restaurants and bars were still full but not quite as crowded and noisy as earlier.

"I can't believe I came all the way down here and the son of a bitch cheated me out of dragging his sorry ass back to Denver. It's hard to let it go."

"Sheriff Clayton will do a good job," Maggie told him. "Anything you can tell him about Gruber will help his investigation."

Glen rubbed at his eyes, only now remembering how exhausted he was. "I suppose the bastard got what was coming to him."

"A wise medical examiner once told me, we die as we live."

"Is that the equivalent of what goes around comes around?"

She smiled and tipped her glass at him, "Touché."

He raised his glass and was about to take a sip when he saw a woman approach the bar. She looked familiar but he couldn't place her. Then he realized who she was. Her hair was shorter. She looked much thinner than when he'd met her over a year ago. But he recognized her walk, the way she handled herself.

"Someone you know," Maggie asked. "Or someone you'd like to know?"

"What? Oh, sorry. No, I think I know her." He sipped his bourbon and continued to watch out of the corner of his eyes. She was at the bar, ordering drinks and laughing with her friends, three women at a table near the bar.

"She's not a blond," Maggie said as if reading his mind. She sat back and took another look. "But even from this distance I'd say the lipstick's a match."

His eyes met Maggie's. She was thinking exactly what he was thinking.

"No such thing as coincidences, right?" he said.

"It's no longer your case," Maggie reminded him. "She wore a wig, probably stole her wineglass and the bottle was wiped down. I checked. They'll never pull DNA off that tissue."

"The least I can do is say hello."

The woman's back was to Glen when he walked up and leaned on the bar. He ordered another round of drinks and watched, waiting for her to notice him. The glance was subtle at first, almost flirtatious.

Then he saw the realization.

"Hello, Mrs. Gruber."

"Detective." She kept her body turned away from him and looked for the bartender. "I'm sorry I don't remember your name."

But he knew she did remember. He told her anyway, "Glen. Glen Karst. Are you here on vacation?"

"We are. Yes, actually we were until the hurricane."

"No other reason you chose Pensacola?" His eyes waited for hers. She met his stare and didn't flinch. Didn't look away. In a split second he thought he could see her confirmation, her admission that she knew exactly what he was talking about. That she knew why he was there and what he had found.

Without a blink she said, "Just having some fun and my friends can vouch for that."

The bartender interrupted with a tray of colorful drinks ready and hovering. Before Mrs. Gruber took them she pulled out a business card from her pocket, hesitated then handed it to Glen.

"I have my own business now," she told him, taking the tray and handing the bartender a fifty dollar bill. "Keep the change, sweetie," she told the young man and without giving Glen another look, she returned to her table and friends.

Glen returned to the high-top with fresh drinks and scooted his chair closer. He placed the business card on the table without looking at it or at Maggie.

"You got lucky. She gave you her number?"

"No, I already have it. What she gave me was a cold shoulder." Glen said. "That's Gruber's ex-wife."

"I think she may have given you more than that," Maggie told him and he looked up to see her reading the business card. She handed it to him and immediately Glen knew.

Elaine Gruber had her own business all right. Making fine jewelry and specializing in gold-plating.

AUTHOR'S NOTE: *A Breath of Hot Air* was first published in 2011 in the anthology, *Florida Heatwave*, edited by Michael Lister. It was written in cooperation with Patricia Bremmer whose Detective Glen Karst appears in several of her novels.

It was also written as a companion piece to my novel, *Damaged*, so although this short story can be enjoyed on its own, there are pieces that go along with the novel that I've carefully tucked in. If you've already read *Damaged* or going to read it, you'll notice some of the following: *(Don't worry, no spoilers.)*

- Maggie is staying on Pensacola Beach at the Hilton and has just spent the day with a Coast Guard helicopter crew (rescue swimmer Elizabeth Bailey and company).
- Hurricane Isaac is barreling up the Gulf, headed for Pensacola.
- A stranger who introduces himself as Joe Black, shares a drink with Detective Glen Karst at the hotel bar. Joe Black plays an important role in *Damaged*.

All of my short stories, novellas and novels can be enjoyed on their own, but because Maggie O'Dell is a reoccurring character in two of my series, I often mention some of the other cases she's worked. The investigation she mentions with the six, young men in a cabin who commit suicide rather than be taken by law enforcement is the beginning to my novel, *The Soul Catcher*.

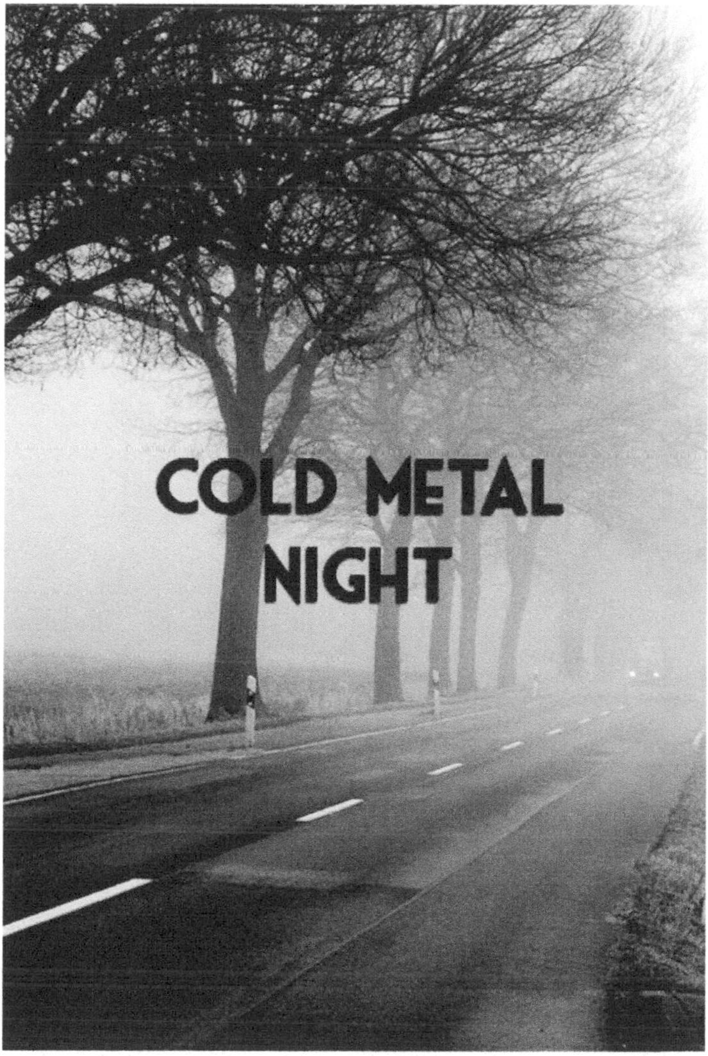
COLD METAL
NIGHT

COLD METAL
NIGHT

CHAPTER 1

Sunday, December 4
2:37 a.m.
Downtown Omaha, Nebraska

NICK MORRELLI STUFFED HIS hands deep inside his pockets.

Damn! It had gotten cold.

And he'd forgotten his gloves. He could see his breath. Air so cold it stung his eyes and hurt to breathe.

Snow crunched beneath his shoes. Italian leather. Salvatore Ferragamo slip-ons. Five hundred and ten dollars. The stupidest purchase he'd ever let his sister, Christine talk him into. They made him look like a mob boss, or worse – a politician – instead of a security expert.

He was at a private party when he got Pete's call. Figured he could easily walk the two blocks from the Flat Iron to the Rockwood Building. But it had been snowing steadily for the last ten hours. Now he treaded carefully over the pile of ice chunks the snowplows left at the curbs. He already almost wiped out twice despite the salt and sand.

City crews were working overtime, trying to clear the streets for Sunday's Holiday of Lights Festival. It was a huge celebration. The beginning of the Christmas season. Live music, carolers, arts and craft events. Performers dressed as Dickens characters would stroll the Old Market's cobblestone streets. The ConAgra Ice Rink would be packed with skaters. Tomorrow night the city would turn on tens of thousands of twinkling white lights that decorated all the trees on the Gene Leahy Mall and strung along the rooftops of the downtown buildings. Even the high-rises.

A festive time and a security nightmare for people like Nick. The company he worked for, United Allied, provided security for a dozen buildings in the area. The Rockwood Building was one of them.

As Nick hurried across Sixteenth Street he glanced up to see the fat, wet flakes glitter against the night sky. It was the kind of stuff he and his sister called magical Christmas dust when they were kids.

Pete was waiting for him at the back door of the Rockwood Building. It was one of Nick's favorites. A historic brick six-story with an atrium in the middle that soared up all six floors. Reminded Nick of walking into an indoor garden, huge green plants and a domed skylight above. The building housed offices, all of them quiet at this time of night, making Pete's job more about caretaking than guarding.

But tonight Pete looked spooked. His eyes were wide. His hair looked a shade whiter against his black skin. He held a nightstick tight in his trembling hands. Nick had never seen the old man like this. He didn't even know Pete owned a nightstick.

"He didn't show up at midnight like usual," Pete was telling Nick as he led him down a hallway. Nick wasn't sure who he was talking about. All he told Nick on the phone was, "please get over here . . . now."

He was taking Nick to another exit, double-wide doors that opened out into an alley. The doors weren't used except by maintenance or housekeeping to haul out the trash.

"He usually stops by. You said it was okay." He shot a look back over his shoulder at Nick but he didn't slow down. "He does a little shoveling if I ask." Pete was out of breath. The nightstick stayed in his right fist. "I made us some hot cocoa tonight. So cold out. When he didn't show up I took a look around."

Pete shoved open the doors, slow and easy, peeking around them like he was expecting someone to jump out at him.

"Pete, you're starting to freak me out." Nick patted him on the shoulder, gently holding him back so he could step around him. "If someone's in trouble, we'll help him out."

After Thanksgiving he had made an executive decision to allow homeless people to sleep in some of the back entries of the buildings he took care of. He told Pete and his other night guards to call him if there was a problem. During the holidays he didn't have the heart to toss them into the street. Most of them didn't cause any problems. They were just looking for someplace to get out of the cold.

Nick took two steps out into the frigid alley and immediately he saw a heap of gray wool and dirty denim in a bloody pile of snow. The man's face was twisted under a bright green and orange argyle scarf that Nick recognized. His stomach fell to his knees.

"Oh God, not Gino. What the hell happened?"

Nick tried to get closer. The damned shoes slipped on a trail of blood that was already icing over. He lost his balance. Started to fall. His hand caught the corner of the Dumpster. Ice-cold metal sliced open his palm but he held on. By now he was breathing hard. Puffs of steam like a dragon. He took a deep breath, planted his feet. Then he reached over to Gino while still gripping the corner of the Dumpster.

Nick pressed two fingers to the man's neck. Gino's skin was almost as cold as the metal of the Dumpster.

CHAPTER 2

4:05 a.m.
Crown Plaza
Kansas City, Missouri

SALSA MUSIC STARTLED Maggie O'Dell awake. She jolt up in bed and scrambled to the edge before she realized it was her phone. She'd accidentally changed the ringtone and had been too exhausted to fix it.

"I think we may have caught a lucky break," the voice said without a greeting.

It was R.J. Tully, her sometimes partner when the FBI sent two instead of one. A rare occasion these days.

She pushed hair out of her eyes, blinked to focus on the red digits of the hotel's alarm clock.

"It better be lucky. You woke me up."

"Aw geez! Sorry. I thought you never sleep."

Tully had to be the only law enforcement officer she knew who said things like "Aw geez and holy crap." It made her smile as she fumbled in the dark to turn on a light.

"Seriously, I didn't think you'd be asleep," he followed up.

He knew she had been battling a stretch of insomnia for over a year now. Getting shot in the head two months ago didn't help matters. Technically it was called a "scraping of the skull alongside the left temporal lobe." Unofficially it hurt like hell and the throbbing pain that still visited her head on a regular basis was a bitch. Otherwise she was okay. At least that's what she kept telling people.

"What's the lucky break?"

"Got a phone call from Omaha. Homeless man. Stabbed. Looks like our guy."

She stood up from the bed, rubbed the sleep from her eyes and started turning on lamps. She'd been in the Kansas City area trying to dig up something, anything. But the victim here, and the evidence, was already two weeks cold.

"What makes them think it's our guy?"

"Blitz attack. No other injuries. Single stab wound to the chest, just under the rib cage. Preliminaries suggest a long, double-edged blade."

That sounded about right.

For four weeks she'd been chasing this guy halfway around the country. It started at the end of October when FBI agent John Baldwin asked her to take a look at a "slice 'n go" down in Nashville. Maggie was still recovering from her own injuries but she owed Baldwin a favor and told him she'd take a look.

Lieutenant Taylor Jackson had sent Maggie every scrap they had on the case, which included witness interviews, security video and even a driver's license. Unfortunately the video footage showed only a flash of white at the bottom of the screen -- the bill of a white ballcap. The driver's license ended up being a deadend, too, although it was an excellent fake. Even the witness interviews didn't turn up anything too interesting except that the man in question "smiled too much."

Just when Maggie believed there wasn't enough to go on something odd happened. Her boss, Assistant Director Raymond Kunze, head of the Behavioral Science Unit at Quantico brought her the case – the exact same case. He insisted she and Tully make it their top priority. Kunze had been sending Tully and her around on wild goose chases for almost a year. Maggie was immediately suspicious. Why this case? What was the political connection? Who did Kunze owe a favor to this time?

She hated that she was right. Turns out the senior senator from Tennessee was a personal friend of the Nashville victim's father. It didn't take much digging for Maggie to discover this wasn't a one-time "slice 'n go." She and Tully had found another two victims in New Orleans. According to NOPD Detective Stacy Killian, both were homeless, one a new mother, the other an elderly man.

Searching ViCAP she discovered what could be as many as ten to twelve victims. Different cities across the country. Similar victims. Same MO. All of them quite possibly the work of one killer she and Tully nicknamed the Night Slicer.

Now Maggie paced the hotel room listening to Tully give her more details. She could hear him rattling paper and knew the notes he had taken were probably on a take-out menu or dry cleaning receipt – his usual notepads, whatever was handy.

"Here's the thing," Tully said. "Omaha's ME thinks this one happened earlier this morning. Internal body temp says within last six hours. Night security guard claims it had to be around two o'clock."

"Two o'clock in the morning? That's only a few hours ago. How can he be so sure?"

"He knows the victim. Says the guy..." more paper shuffling. "Says Gino usually picked up a dozen extras of the *Sunday Omaha World Herald* right off the dock. He'd sell them on the street to make a few bucks. But first, he'd bring the security guard a copy and they'd drink hot chocolate."

"That sounds all very nice but since when do we determine time of death from a security guard's Sunday morning ritual?"

"Thing is, they found him between two-thirty and three this morning. He already had his dozen newspapers. The Sunday edition didn't hit the dock until two-o-five."

Tully went silent. He was waiting for it to settle in, and Maggie finally understood the lucky break.

"So we've got a fresh kill," she said. And then the realization hit her. "And less than twenty-four hours before he slices number two and leaves town."

"Omaha's about 180 miles from Kansas City. Just a hop up and a skip down. Twenty, thirty minute flight," Tully said. "Might be some delays. Sounds like there's a bunch of new snow."

"I have a rental. I'll drive." She hated flying. Tully's "hop up and skip down" already had her stomach flipping. "It'll probably be quicker than trying to get a flight, getting to the airport, going through security."

"Looks like a three hour drive, but in the snow—"

"No problem."

"You sure?"

"You worry too much. I'll exchange my rental car for an SUV. Let Omaha know I'm on my way."

CHAPTER 3

5:41 a.m.
The Old Market, Embassy Suites

HE LOOKED OUT HIS HOTEL suite's window and down on the empty cobblestone streets. Earlier there had been horses and carriages, street performers on a couple of the corners. The brick buildings used to be warehouses on the Missouri River but now housed restaurants and specialty shops.

Last night despite the snow, the sidewalks had been filled with people, the streets busy with traffic. There had even been a patrol officer on horseback. And yet just five, six blocks away he had been able to slide a blade up into a man's heart and walk away. In fact, he walked back through the hustle and bustle to his hotel without a single person noticing.

All was good. He was back in his groove. That nagging fury would no longer drive him to make reckless mistakes.

New Orleans had set him off track. Then Nashville really screwed him up. He had always been careful about choosing targets no one would miss. But Heath Stover, a blast from the past, had knocked him way off his game. And so did that girl, that rich bitch pretending to be some lost soul. The news media continued to cover her murder but at least they were calling it just another unfortunate incident. Just another of a long list of crimes besieging the Occupy camps across the country.

That's the word a reporter used, "besieging," like the protesters were soldiers in dugouts coming under attack. He shook his head at that. He was sick of seeing the protesters in every city he traveled to. Thankfully, he hadn't had to deal with any of them in Kansas City or here in Omaha. Another good sign that he was finally back on track.

And why shouldn't he be back on top of his world? Sales were up. Bosco's new laser-guided scalpel was a huge hit. Omaha's medical mecca was like putty in his hands on Thursday and Friday at the Quest Center conference. He had exploded past his sales quota.

Still, it had taken this morning's kill to completely renew his confidence.

He looked around the suite and rubbed his hands together. Checked his watch. Maybe he would shower, dress and go down for the breakfast buffet. He had the whole day off. He didn't have to leave until tomorrow morning. Tonight he was looking forward to the Holiday of Lights festivities. The Old Market would be filled with people again and sounds of the seasons. Now with his newfound confidence he wouldn't need to go far at all to find target number two.

CHAPTER 4

7:59 a.m.
Omaha Police Headquarters

NICK MORRELLI CRUSHED the paper cup and tossed it into the corner wastebasket. He'd had enough coffee. He was tired. He wanted to go home. He rubbed his eyes and paced the room, a poor excuse for an employee lounge with a metal table and folding chairs, a row of vending machines, coffee maker and a sagging sofa along the back wall.

The door opened and his captor came in, shirt sleeves rolled up, shaved head shiny with perspiration. Detective Tommy Pakula handed Nick a black and white print-out. It was a copy of a driver's license.

"Do you recognize this guy? Maybe seen him around any of your properties?"

The license had been enlarged which only made the photo blurred. The guy looked pretty ordinary, could be anybody.

"No, I don't think so."

Pakula sat down in one of the folding chairs. Pointed to one across the table for Nick to sit down. They'd already done this. What more could he ask? But Nick sat down. Tommy Pakula was one of the good guys. Four daughters. Still married to his high school sweetheart. Nick had been questioned by him before a couple years ago. Another case. Another killer.

"You were a sheriff not so long ago," Pakula said, getting Nick's attention.

That was true. Nick had been a county sheriff. Got his fill after a killer almost claimed his nephew as his next victim.

Just when Nick thought Pakula might finally cut him some slack, the man came in with another verbal punch. "You should know better. So tell me again why you thought you should be touching this dead guy before you called us?"

"If he wasn't dead I wanted to help him."

Pakula raised an eyebrow.

"It's Gino," Nick said in almost a whisper.

He watched Pakula sit back, pull in a long deep breath. Rubbed his jaw.

Everybody loved Gino. Nobody knew his last name but he was a familiar face downtown, part of the landscape. Years ago he used to sell Italian sausage and peppers out of a rickety stand he'd set up on the corner of Sixteenth and Douglas, right in front of the Brandeis Building. Suddenly he was living on the streets. Tall, thin – a little bent over as he grew older – with friendly brown eyes that sparkled despite his situation. Security guards and police officers took care of him. Even the guys on the newspaper's loading dock gave him twelve papers every Sunday morning for him to sell and buy himself a hot breakfast that wasn't one provided by a local shelter. They all loved Gino. Took care of him. But they hadn't taken care of him last night.

"Is this the guy you think stabbed Gino?" Nick held up the print-out.

Pakula nodded. "FBI thinks so, too. He's done it in other cities. We've been keeping an eye out ever since he hit Kansas City about two weeks ago."

"Mind if I keep this?"

"Go ahead. Maybe check with your security people. You said your company has how many buildings downtown?"

"Nine. Plus three in the Old Market."

Nick folded the print-out. Tucked it in the back pocket of his trousers. He'd get this bastard himself if he had to. Then he tried to decide if he should tell Pakula that the Rockwood Building had security cameras on every corner. Before he decided, the door to the lounge opened again and a young cop stuck his head inside.

"Sorry to interrupt. A woman's here to see you, Detective Pakula. Insisted I tell you that she brought you doughnuts all the way from Kansas City?"

The young cop's face flushed a bit, like he wasn't sure if he should be delivering what sounded like a personal message.

Pakula smiled and stood up. "Send her in here."

The cop disappeared. Pakula shot Nick a look. Another smile.

"FBI," he said. "First time I met her I was eating a doughnut. Had a cup of coffee in my other hand." He shook his head, but the grin hadn't left yet. "She'll never stop busting my chops about that."

Nick should have figured it out, but he was totally surprised when the lounge door opened again and Maggie O'Dell walked in, carrying a white bakery box that she meant as a joke for Pakula. From the look on her face when she saw Nick, he figured the joke was probably on her. But only for a second or two.

"Nick Morrelli," she said. "I haven't seen you since you drove off with that blond bomb expert in Minneapolis."

Nick winced. Damn, she was good.

CHAPTER 5

10:57 p.m.
The Rockwood Building

THE LAST TIME MAGGIE had worked with Nick Morrelli they spent hours watching security footage. Mall of America. The day after Thanksgiving. Black Friday became bloody Friday. Three college kids set off backpacks filled with explosives.

Here they were again, sitting in a small room in front of a wall of computer monitors.

"How's Timmy and Christine?" she asked. She and Nick had a history that went back further than Minneapolis. They'd worked on a serial killer case when Nick was sheriff. And again, years later when the killer returned.

"Timmy's playing football this year. Christine's good."

They sat side by side in captain's chairs like pilots in a cockpit. Pakula would join them in a half hour or so.

"How's your doctor?" Nick asked, keeping his eyes on the computer monitors but unsuccessful in keeping the sarcasm out of his voice.

Instead of telling him that Benjamin Platt was not hers, she simply said, "Ben's good."

She refrained from asking whatever happened to the blond bomb expert. That was more than a year ago. She knew Nick probably didn't remember the woman's name anymore. And there lied the reason that she had never seriously considered a relationship with Nick Morrelli. Simply put – he wasn't relationship material. Maggie had too much drama in her professional life to put up with it in her personal life.

But charming, yes. Handsome – God, he was still gorgeous. Tall, dark and handsome with blue eyes. He had managed to keep his college quarterback physique. She didn't deny that there had been chemistry between the two of them. Just sitting next to him she could still feel it. Annoying as hell.

She tried to turn her attention to the monitors. She was exhausted from lack of sleep. Her back was tight and tense from a slippery three-hour drive in a small rental car because everyone else had the good sense of renting the SUV's before the snow hit. Somehow she needed to focus.

She pulled up the chair. Planted her elbows on the table in front of her.

"Who are you this week?" she said aloud to the computer monitor, like the Night Slicer might answer.

"Pakula gave me a copy of the driver's license."

"That's all we have."

"You think he changes his appearance?"

"He must, but I'm guessing it's subtle. He definitely changes his name. He has a normal life somewhere. I think he travels the country on business. Different cities. A new group of people each time who don't know him. We have that picture from the driver's license out to every metropolitan police department. We haven't gotten a hit yet."

"But you've been tracking him?"

"Only by his victims. And his M.O. He's right-handed. Uses a double-edged stiletto. At least seven inches long. He does a blitz attack. It's probably no more than an incidental bump. Slips the blade in just under the breastbone where he knows he won't have any bone chattering. The angle of the knife is interesting."

"So somehow he knows exactly where to stab?"

"Yes, it appears so."

She glanced at Nick while he tapped buttons on a keyboard. He started the film footage from a camera labeled: Northwest corner of Rockwood.

"His image was captured on a security camera at the Tennessee Performing Arts Center," Maggie continued. "Actually it was only his back but it was enough to give us some idea of how tall he is compared to his victim. He has to angle the blade—"

She pushed out her chair and stood. "It's probably easier if I show you." Fact was she was too exhausted to talk about it. He glanced up at her, paused the monitors and stood up in front of her.

She grabbed a ballpoint pen from the table and held it in her right hand the same way she believed the Night Slicer did.

"He holds it low. Probably has the stiletto up his sleeve until he needs it." She stepped closer. "He always slips it in just below the rib cage." She put her left hand flat against Nick's abdomen to show him where and immediately she realized this was a mistake when she felt him shiver under her touch. Her eyes met his and she felt the heat rush to her face.

Thankfully exhaustion pushed her into professional mode. She took a step back as she moved her hand with the pen and her arm in the same motion the killer must use.

"He shoves the knife in at an upward angle. Usually pierces the heart. Sometimes the lungs. Sometimes both."

Finished with the show and tell, she avoided his eyes and took her seat again. Waited for him to do the same. He was slow about joining her and she wanted to kick herself. There was obvious still too much between them. She glanced over at him. Wanted to tell him she couldn't afford any of the emotion she was seeing in his face right now.

"Gino was a good guy," he said, surprising her. "He didn't deserve to die this way."

She was wrong. The emotion wasn't about her. Maybe she was a little disappointed that it wasn't about her.

"He's been killing two victims in each city. Usually within a period of twenty-four hours." Maggie sat back. Ran her fingers through her hair. "Then he disappears. Gone. Like he never existed." She looked at her wristwatch. "In less than fifteen hours he's going to kill someone else."

CHAPTER 6

1:39 p.m.
The Old Market

HE HAD BEEN WATCHING the old woman for over an hour. He followed her around but kept to the shadows and back far enough away that she never noticed him. Though he wondered if she noticed much of anything around her.

He'd gotten close enough to hear her muttering. Not just talking to herself but arguing as if with some invisible friend. She had abandoned her shopping cart behind a Dumpster, tucking it away to hide it as best as she could. The snow made it too difficult for her to move it over the crusted piles left by the snowplows. He almost helped her once. Wanting to touch the fringe of her gray knit hat and feel whether the fringe was part of the hat or actually her hair.

Her territory seemed to be within the Old Market area. Interesting, since he didn't see any other homeless people here, venturing around the cobblestone district. He watched as she wandered the streets quite fascinated by things no one else saw. Once he saw her stop abruptly in the middle of the sidewalk and wave pedestrians around her to avoid stepping on something smashed in the snow. No one else stopped to give it a look. Most people ignored her or scowled and went wide.

That's when he realized she had to be the next one.

She was perfect. Someone no one would miss. She was virtually invisible to these bastards. Even as they were forced to walk around her, they still didn't seem to notice her. No one cared to stop and see what it was that she was protecting, what she found that was so precious and fascinating that she insisted they walk around it.

And suddenly he couldn't wait. He wanted to cut her right now. Right here in the freezing cold sunny daylight. Right in the middle of the crowd that couldn't see her.

Except he hadn't brought his knife.

And so, he'd wait until tonight though his fingers fidgeted with anticipation.

He walked toward her. She was bent over now, touching the object. He decided he couldn't resist. He needed to walk close enough just to see what it was. Then he'd be content to go back to his hotel suite and wait. He already knew where he could find her.

As he got closer he saw her wrapping her ragged knit gloves around the object that had captured her attention and sent her into such a protective mode. What in the world could have captured her attention? Someone's wallet? No, there was a sparkle. Cradled in her hands the sunlight glinted off of it. Perhaps someone's lost jewelry?

He slowed down as he approached. A couple more steps and he was able to see her precious keepsake. The object was a long icicle. Dozens of others hung above from the awning that stretched halfway over the sidewalk. An icicle. *A frickin' icicle.*

He smiled to himself as he passed by and glanced at her. Her eyes flitted up to meet his and he wanted to tell her that he'd see her later. That it would be his pleasure to watch the surprise in those same eyes as her life spilled out of her.

CHAPTER 7

4:57 pm
Downtown Omaha

IT WAS ALREADY GETTING DARK by the time Maggie and Detective Pakula started walking the streets. There were crowds gathered at the ice rink and around the outdoor mall that stretched several city blocks long. Tonight was the lighting ceremony when hundreds of thousands of lights in trees and bushes and along rooftops would be turned on, marking the beginning of the holiday season.

"We've pulled in everybody on this, looking and talking to people since five this morning," he told her as they strolled the cobblestone streets, looking more like an old married couple than a couple of cops.

Pakula wore an old camouflage parka but nothing on his shaved head. Maggie kept on her leather jacket and added a red Huskers ballcap that Pakula had given her.

"It'll help you fit in," he told her about the cap.

She didn't argue. She was getting restless. Exhaustion had given way to the adrenaline that had taken over. Too much time had passed. Why did she ever believe they'd find this guy? It was like looking for a needle in a haystack.

She and Nick had wasted two whole hours pouring over the security tapes only to come up empty handed. At one point they saw Gino enter the frame. According to Nick it looked like he was headed around the corner to the front door where he always came to meet Pete, the Rockwood Building's night security guard.

But then Gino stopped and turned as if someone had called to him. The camera didn't record sound. They watched Gino cock his head. He grinned and said something before walking back in the direction of whoever had stopped him. He disappeared from the frame. Maggie didn't say it but she knew Gino had most likely headed right over to his killer.

Nick was taking this man's death personally and she didn't quite understand. Maybe it was because it happened outside one of his buildings. He had wanted to come with her and Pakula but they stopped him. He told them he had a license to carry. Pakula told him to go get his hand looked at.

"You should have had stitches," the detective told him, pointing to the wrapped hand that Maggie had noticed immediately but stopped herself from asking about. "You already bloodied up one of my crime scenes."

Pakula bought a hot chocolate for Maggie and a coffee for himself. The steam felt good on her frozen cheeks. She wrapped her hands around the cardboard cup and let it warm her fingers. She only had thin knit gloves. Why did she always come to this part of the country unprepared for the weather?

"You two married?" An old woman came up from behind them. She was trying to push a shopping cart filled with an odd assortment of junk.

"No, we're not married to each other." Pakula answered. "How are you doing tonight? Do you have someplace warm to stay tonight?"

The woman didn't look like she heard him. Instead she muttered something to herself. She struggled to hike the cart over the curb that was still snow covered. Pakula grabbed the front end and lifted it easily onto the sidewalk for her.

"They've got some extra beds over at Saint Gabriel's," he tried again.

This time she blew out a raspberry at him. "I don't need no Saint Gabriel. Lydia and I have been taking care of each other for years."

Both Pakula and Maggie looked around at the same time, looking for someone named Lydia. There was obviously no one with this woman. People went around them, even stepping into the street to do so.

"Do you need me to help you find Lydia?" Pakula asked.

This time the woman stared directly into his eyes, her brow creasing under her dirty gray cap. She looked from him to Maggie then back at Pakula.

"You a cop?" she whispered.

Pakula was good but Maggie heard him clear his throat to cover his surprise.

"It's okay," the old woman reassured him, her face softening. She reached up and touched his arm, almost a grandmotherly gesture. "We've all heard about Gino." She shook her head. "A damned shame." Then she straightened and waved her hand like she was swatting at a fly. "Oh stop it, Lydia. You know who Gino was."

Pakula looked over at Maggie and raised his eyebrows.

The woman probably shouldn't be left on the streets. She obviously needed help but Maggie liked her feistiness and her spirit. As long as she had the shopping cart she was probably safe from their killer. He'd never be able to bump and slice her without having the click-clanking of that shopping cart in the way. It would draw too much attention.

Pakula was pulling out what looked like a business card. He handed it to the old woman.

"You know Danny at the coffee shop on the corner?"

Another raspberry but she took the card. "My God, who doesn't know Danny. That son of a bitch will talk your damned ear off. I take the coffee he gives me just to shut him up."

"You need anything," Pakula insisted, "You hand Danny that card and have him call me."

"What would I need? Me and Lydia we got everything we need right here." She tapped the shopping cart and the contents clanked and shifted.

They watched her rat-tat-tat down the street.

Maggie shook her head when Pakula glanced over at her.

"You can't lock them up," she told him. Though it would be easier to protect them if they were behind bars.

They started walking again. Past Vivace's and the aroma of garlic and warm bread made Maggie's stomach groan. She tried to remember the last time she had eaten. A doughnut that morning in the rental car. No wonder she was running low on energy. She sipped the rest of her hot chocolate.

"And there's another sorry ass," Pakula pointed to the homeless man in the ragged long black coat at the corner. "What am I going to do with these people?"

But as the man turned, both she and Pakula recognized him at the same time.

"What the hell are you doing here?" It was Maggie who posed the question.

Nick Morrelli spun around to face them. With a five o'clock shadow and a torn felt hat with the brim pulled down he looked like a street performer instead of the homeless man he thought he was portraying.

He simply shrugged at her and said, "You're not the boss of me." Then he jumped out into the street causing cars to brake and honk. He ran down the other sidewalk without looking back.

CHAPTER 8

6:15 p.m.
The Old Market

HE HAD THE KNIFE WITH HIM, the cold metal tucked up into his sleeve.

The old woman had the cart with her again.

Damn! But she was so cute. Pulling crap like that on him.

In weeks past it would have made him angry, but his confidence was soaring again. And it didn't matter. He had ruled her out in just the last hour. He had a new target.

The guy reminded him of himself. A pathetic shadow of himself. That long dirty black coat that once upon a time was probably his power coat. Good looking guy, young. In good physical shape. Or at least he had been. Maybe he had been on the fast-track to success. Not anymore. Somewhere along the line he had stumbled big-time.

He followed the guy for a while and knew the man was plastered or flying high. He'd listened to him talk to several people. He made less sense than the old woman with her imaginary friend. No, this guy would probably be thanking him for doing him the service of putting him out of his misery.

Even earlier when the married couple had stopped the guy. They seemed to recognize him. Or thought they did. The man danced around. Slung out some curses. Then he ran off, almost getting run over in the street. He was hilarious. A total loser. Nobody would miss this fool.

He watched him. Studied him. The streets were filling up with people. On one corner there was a four-piece band, or rather four teenagers with instruments, clanging out their version of Christmas songs. Horse-drawn carriages were keeping busy, too. Police horse patrol was back. Same as last night. The lighting ceremony had taken place about fifteen minutes ago and everywhere he looked he was bedazzled by tiny, twinkling white lights.

It was frickin' beautiful. What a lovely night to die.

He stepped out of a doorwell and found his target leaning against a rail, his back to an alley.

He'd have to do him from behind. Not a problem. He knew where to insert the blade. Not in the middle. It'd ram against the spinal cord. It would need to be off to the side. Down below. He'd keep the same angle up. The back tissue would require more pressure but the blade was long enough. He'd still puncture the heart. The only thing he'd miss was meeting the guy's eyes. Seeing the realization there.

Oh well. Sometimes he had to change up a little.

He headed in the other direction where he knew he could go around and up that alley. Soon, buddy. I'll take you out of your misery.

CHAPTER 9

6:18 p.m.

PAKULA HAD TO LEAVE Maggie after a phone call from one of his officers. He thought he may have found the Night Slicer. A desk clerk at the Embassy Suites claimed she recognized the driver's license photo when the officer showed it to her. She said it looked a lot like the guy she checked in on Thursday.

She remembered him because she had complained about her bursitis and he gave her instructions of how long to keep a heating pad on it followed by ice. His remedy really worked and she was pretty sure he must be some kind of doctor. According to the clerk, he was booked through tomorrow morning. The officer was waiting for Pakula before they paid him a visit.

Pakula promised to call her. She wanted to be there if this was their guy. But it seemed too easy. Was it possible he'd be sitting in a hotel suite within ten blocks of where he'd killed Gino?

Maggie decided to backtrack and see if she could find Nick and talk some sense into him. She saw the old woman with her shopping cart set aside. The woman was staring at something in the snow along the side of a building. She seemed fixated on it even to the point of shooing people to take a wide circle around.

Then Maggie saw Nick.

He sat on a rail that in warmer weather probably allowed bike riders to chain up their bikes. His feet dangled. His head wobbled to the music from the street corner behind him. Sometimes the foot traffic got too close and brushed against him, sending his whole body teetering. No one seemed to notice him. Even when they jostled him or bumped him. He was playing his role very well.

She knew if she waved at him he'd ignore her. So instead, she started to walk toward him, walking against a crowd. She weaved her way through, taking her time and putting up with the occasion bump.

This is how he does it, she thought. And suddenly she knew he was here. She could feel him. Gut instinct. It had never failed her.

She looked at the faces coming toward her. Her arms came up across her chest and she walked like she was chilled and not paranoid that a knife would find its way into her chest. The flow of the crowd continued. She found herself pushed along the wall. And suddenly she felt a stab in her back. She spun around. But it was an elbow, not a knife.

Paranoid. She needed to stop.

Through a hole in the crowd she could see Nick, smiling, singing with the music. He was still sitting on the rail. Only now she saw a man coming out of the alley behind him. Well dressed. Alone. White ballcap. Focused on Nick. Walking directly toward Nick. His right arm down at his side.

Oh, God, she could see the flash of metal.

She started pushing her way through the crowd.

"Nick, behind you."

But her voice got drowned out in the noises of the street, the music, the crowd, the traffic. She shoved at bodies. Got shoved back a couple of times.

"FBI," she yelled but nobody moved out of the way for the crazy woman in the red Huskers ballcap.

She tore at her jacket's zipper and yanked at her revolver. Ripped at the clasp to her shoulder holster.

Damn it!

The man was within three feet of Nick.

She waved her arms at him and finally he saw her. He waved back. Smiled. Then he tumbled forward, face down into the snow with the man falling on top of him. Even before she got there she could see the snow turning red.

"Oh God, no."

Then she saw the old woman. She pointed to the stiletto knife still clutched in the dead man's hand.

"That's the bastard that killed Gino," was all she said.

That's when Maggie saw the wide end of an icicle sticking out of the man's back.

CHAPTER 10

10:00 a.m.
Monday, December 5
Embassy Suites

MAGGIE HAD GOTTEN five hours of sleep. For once she felt more than rested. She pulled on a pair of jeans and a favorite warm, bulky sweater and headed down to the lobby. Pakula already had a table. She saw him through the glass elevator. The same elevator John Robert Gunderson aka the Night Slicer had used for the last four days.

"I ordered our coffee," Pakula said, standing when she came to the table and pointing to the can of Diet Pepsi in Maggie's spot. She was impressed that he remembered her wake-up drink.

He had file folders piled up but pushed to the side of the table. She added one to his stack, information Tully had faxed to her late last night.

"So is Gunderson even his real name?" Pakula wanted to know.

"Yes."

They had found a small case inside his hotel suite that contained about a dozen driver's licenses and credit cards with various aliases. All the same initials.

"He's a traveling salesman," she said, taking a sip of the Diet Pepsi. "One of Bosco Blades top salesmen."

"Blades." Pakula shook his head. "Unbelievable."

"He flunked out of med school. I suspected he might have a medical background. He knew too much about where to stab. I just talked to Lieutenant Taylor Jackson this morning. Turns out one of his victims was a classmate of his. Heath Stover. He killed him in Nashville. We think he probably didn't want anyone to know he'd flunked out.

"Also, we now know he was in Nashville for a medical conference. Was supposed to do a presentation but canceled. We think he ran into Stover at the conference. Didn't expect to meet up with anyone who knew him or knew his past. Detective Killian told me there was a medical convention going on in New Orleans when he killed his two victims there. Kansas City was a conference for surgeons. And in Omaha—"

"The sales conference at the Quest Center," Pakula said, making the connection. "For medical devices or something, right?"

She nodded.

"How could he get away with it? Wouldn't his co-workers suspect something?"

"He worked out of a home office. Had a secretary at Bosco that he communicated with by phone, text and email. He met with his boss once a month. And he made all his travel arrangements on his own, so he could be whoever he wanted to be when he was on the road."

"He looked like an ordinary guy," Pakula said. "Best disguise there is."

"What about the old woman? You're not going to press charges are you?"

"Hell no. She did us a favor. I did get her off the streets."

"How did you manage that?"

"I know a guy who handles security for about a dozen buildings in the downtown area. Seems he was able to find a nice little apartment for her in one of them."

Maggie smiled. Of course Nick Morrelli would want to take good care of the woman who saved his life.

"And what about Lydia?" she asked.

"Yeah, Lydia will be there with her. It appears this building even takes cats."

No one realized until last night that the old woman had an old calico cat that she kept bundled up and warm in the shopping cart.

"I've got to head out," Pakula gathered up his file folders and Maggie stood to walk him out before she went back up to the room. "Sure you can't stay for a day or two? My wife makes some of the best kolaches you'll ever eat."

"Maybe next time."

He shook her hand then muttered, "Aw the hell with it," and gave her a hug.

Just as he got to the door, Nick Morrelli came in. The two men exchanged greetings and then Nick's eyes found her.

He was clean-shaven this morning and dressed in crisp trousers and a bright red ski jacket. She stood in the archway to the restaurant area where only a few tables were occupied at this time on a Monday morning. She waited for him, watched him stride across the lobby. Last night when she thought he had been stabbed she had such a mix of emotions. Nick had a way of doing that to her.

He wasn't relationship material, she reminded herself as he got closer and she couldn't pull her eyes away from his. He had called early this morning, asking if they could spend some time together. Maybe go ice skating. Take a carriage ride. She had agreed. Now as she got a whiff of his aftershave she wondered if perhaps that wasn't such a wise decision.

He pointed to something over her head.

"You're always giving me mixed signals, Maggie O'Dell," he told her.

She looked up to see the mistletoe hanging high above her in the archway. Before she could say a word he was kissing her. And suddenly she found herself thinking it might just be too cold to leave the hotel.

AUTHOR'S NOTE: Cold Metal Night was first published in 2011 in Slices of Night, an novella written in three parts with co-authors J.T. Ellison an Erica Spindler

ELECTRIC
BLUE

ELECTRIC BLUE

CHAPTER 1

**Gulf of Mexico,
Pensacola, Florida**

FBI AGENT MAGGIE O'DELL STARED at the helicopter. She stood so close she could feel the vibration of the engine even as it idled. The soft, slow whir of the blades already made her nauseated though she could barely hear them with the gusts of wind. She watched the crew methodically run through the last of their flight checks and she still couldn't believe she had agreed to this.

It had been a year since her last excursion, and she had promised herself never ever again to set foot inside another helicopter. Yet here she was. All decked out in a flight suit. It was red-orange, what she knew the Coasties affectionately called "mustangs." The suits were designed to provide flotation and were also fire retardant. Neither of which added much comfort to Maggie. This time her suit was

complete with a helmet with ICS (internal commu-
nication system). The ICS was a step up. Last time
they didn't let her communicate with them.

She glanced over at her partner, R.J. Tully. He
stood back about a hundred feet from the helipad
where he'd be safe and sound from the downwash
when they lifted off. He gave her a forced grin and a
thumbs-up. Maggie still felt like she had gotten the
short straw, though of course, they hadn't drawn
straws. They were professionals. Although standing
here with cockroaches gnawing inside her stomach
she might offer Tully rock/paper/scissors or a toss
of a coin and not care how childish it sounded. But
she had been up with this aircrew before. Somehow
that made her win – or lose – depending on one's
perspective.

She needed to block out how the clouds had
turned day into dusk though it was barely noon.
Was that a raindrop she felt? How much longer before
the sky burst open? She needed to stay focused and
concentrate on the reason she and Tully were here.

A United States senator's family was missing –
somewhere out at sea. Maggie and Tully's boss, Assistant Director Raymond Kunze – who never met a
politician he couldn't be manipulated by – had sent
his two agents to play fetch.

Okay, that wasn't at all how Kunze had worded
it, of course, but that was what it felt like to Maggie
and Tully.

Kunze had been sending the two of them on
odd missions for about two years now. And just
when Maggie thought the shelf life on his reign of
punishment would expire, he came up with yet another assignment or errand.

The storm added urgency to their mission. Maggie and Tully had barely escaped DC before the snow began falling. But they hadn't escaped the storm front. The monster system looped all the way down from the Midwest to the Panhandle of Florida then back up the eastern coastline.

Down here in Florida it was only just beginning, taking the form of angry, black thunderheads. It had rained all the way from the airport. Seventeen to twenty inches were predicted during the next forty-eight hours. They were in a lull. In the distance Maggie could hear a rumble of thunder, a reminder that the calm would not last long. As if on cue, the pilot, Lieutenant Commander Wilson, gestured for her to hurry up and come aboard. Then he climbed inside.

Liz Bailey, the rescue swimmer, and Pete Kesnik, the flight mechanic, both waited for her at the cabin door. Bailey had already slipped Maggie a couple of capsules when no one was watching. She had done this favor for Maggie the last time even before she knew her. Who would have guessed it would become a ritual.

The capsules were a concoction of ginger and other herbs that magically quelled her nausea. Maggie dry-swallowed them now. Then she put on her flight helmet and climbed into the helicopter.

CHAPTER 2

THE WIND WHIPPED AND SHOVED at the Coast Guard H-65 Helo. Bruise-colored clouds threatened to burst. Maggie could see flickers of lightning rippling through the mass that, thankfully, continued to stay in the distance for now. But it was definitely moving their way. It looked like the storm was rolling in on waves of clouds and in layers of gray and purple. Below, the gulf water swirled and churned up white caps.

Sane people would be starting to take shelter, moving inland and grounding their flights in preparation for the storm. Wind gusts of forty to sixty miles per hour were predicted along with the rain. Yet, this aircrew had not flinched at the order to take flight.

Within fifteen minutes they found what they believed to be the senator's houseboat. Maggie knew from the file she and Tully had been given that the boat was eighteen feet wide by seventy-five feet long. It was a luxury widebody named *Electric Blue* and worth almost a half million dollars. From two-hundred feet above it looked like a toy rocking and rolling in a sea of boiling water.

Maggie watched Liz Bailey prepare to deploy. No one else appeared to think this was an absolutely crazy idea. Wilson and his co-pilot, Tommy Ellis, couldn't keep the helicopter from pitching one way and jerking the other as they tried to hover above the boat. And yet, Bailey was going to leap out into the gusts, tethered to the helicopter by a single cable. Maggie had watched her do it before but it still astonished her. Was it bravery or insanity?

Maggie had been impressed with the young woman from the moment they met. Liz – Elizabeth Bailey, AST3, RS (rescue swimmer) – was a Coastie veteran at twenty-eight years old. She had told Maggie stories about how she had scraped her knees on sinking rooftops during Katrina and waded through debris-filled sewage left by Isaac. Despite having more rescues than many of her male counterparts Bailey was still considered a novelty, a rare breed, one of less than a dozen women to pass the rigorous training and earn the title "rescue swimmer."

That was one thing she and Maggie had in common. Both of them had clawed their way to garnering respect in fields that were still male dominated. But Bailey had done so under extreme circumstances, propelling herself out into the elements, literally hanging by what Maggie considered a thread. Having watched her do that a few times, Maggie was convinced she had the less dangerous job of hunting killers.

Now Bailey was ready. She sidled up to the cabin door but she had put off changing out her flight helmet with ICS for her Seda swim helmet. Maggie knew she was waiting while her aircrew tried to assess the situation below. Once she switched out helmets she would no longer be able to communicate with them except through hand signals.

"No one's responding," Tommy Ellis, their copilot said. He had been trying to make radio contact with the houseboat.

"Keep trying," Lt. Commander Wilson told him. "Who the hell takes a houseboat out in the Gulf of Mexico with a monster storm in the forecast?"

"It was supposed to be just a few thunderstorms," Pete Kesnick said, while he checked the cables.

Kesnick, the flight mechanic was also the hoist operator. Maggie remembered that he was the senior member of this aircrew with fifteen or sixteen years, all of them at Air Station Mobile.

"Ever been on one before?" Kesnick asked no one in particular. "Like a floating condo. Pretty sweet." He adjusted and worked the cables that would lower Bailey down.

Wilson slid back his flight helmet's visor and turned to look at Bailey. He waited for her eyes before he said, "I don't like this. Dispatch claims six on board. We can't rouse anyone and I sure as hell don't see anybody."

The last time Maggie had been on board with this crew the men had all but ignored Bailey. Sometime during a nasty rescue flight in the vicious outer bands of Hurricane Isaac, Maggie had watched this same aircrew go from calling Liz Bailey *the* rescue swimmer" to *our* rescue swimmer." She was glad to see the attitude had stuck.

From what Maggie knew there had been no distress call from the boat. That was one of the reasons the senator had gone into full panic mode. And Wilson was right. Maggie couldn't see anyone down below. Empty lounge chairs and a putting green that looked the size of a postage stamp occupied the upper deck. The lower one couldn't be seen from above, but if anyone was on board and the radio was out, they'd be coming out into view, at least, to take a look at the noise above.

Instead, the houseboat thrashed around as waves pummeled against its sides. It made no attempt to escape or retreat. Maggie was definitely no expert but she couldn't help wondering if the engines had been turned off and the steering house abandoned. Interior lights could be seen, but may have been automatically powered on by the darkening sky.

"It's your call, Bailey," Wilson finally said. "What say you?"

CHAPTER 3

R.J. TULLY THOUGHT HE HAD THE EASY part of this assignment until he met Senator Ellie Delanor Ramos.

She had asked to meet him in the parking lot under Pensacola Beach's famous beach ball water tower. Most of the spaces were empty. Still, he chose a corner closest to the water. He had seen the junior senator from Florida in newspaper photos and on television news. She had become an outspoken proponent for immigration reform though pundits were always quick to point out that her own ancestry traced back to the Mayflower. She was hardly the poster child for such an endeavor and even her physical presence seemed to highlight that fact.

A strikingly beautiful woman in her forties, her skin was creamy white, her eyes a bright blue. She wore her mane of caramel-colored hair loose and just long enough to brush her shoulders when she walked. As Tully watched her cross the parking lot, flanked by two men, he understood immediately why this woman was regarded as one of the most powerful women in Washington, D.C. She carried herself not at all like the model or beauty queen that she looked like, but rather a Fortune 500 CEO, one capable of shoving aside or destroying anything – or anyone – who might stand in her way.

"You must Agent Tully," she said with her hand outstretched to him from four feet away.

"That's correct, Senator." Her grip was firm, long fingers, nails painted a blood red.

"For God's sake, call me Ellie."

"Are you sure?"

"Absolutely. Do you prefer R.J. or Agent Tully?"

"Actually just Tully is fine."

He glanced at the two men who accompanied her. No introductions were expected. Both men stood silent and a foot behind her. Secret service? Bodyguards? They wore dark suits and sunglasses despite the gray sky. They looked more like federal agents than Tully did.

"I missed the helicopter?" she asked an obvious question immediately betraying her cool, calm façade.

"I'm afraid so."

"Any news?"

It had been less than thirty minutes. And Tully was certain the senator would be alerted of any news long before he would, just like she knew the helicopter had already left.

Instead of answering and wasting time with pleasantries, he said, "Sheriff Langley said there was someplace you wanted me to check out."

"Yes, but I don't want that idiot going along."

So much for pleasantries. "Sheriff Langley?"

"If I thought the locals could handle this I wouldn't have asked Raymond for his assistance."

"Raymond," Tully realized was FBI Assistant Director Kunze – his boss. It sounded odd having someone call him by his first name. A little like calling Hitler, "Adolf." It made Tully even more uncomfortable going over the heads of local law enforcement. This was their turf, their territory. Forget about pissing contests. Usually it made sense to have them leading the way, or at least along for the ride. Local law enforcement had the contacts. They knew the players as well as the shortcuts. It saved time. Mostly, it spared Tully from a lot of headaches. But this was a United States senator. Both he and Maggie had been told to "assist her" in any way possible that would return her family safely ashore.

"Where is it that you want me check?"

"A friend of my husband's." She hesitated, looking for a correct word. "Not really a friend. More of a business associate."

"What exactly to do you think happened here?"

She glanced back at the two men. "Can we have some privacy, please?"

The bigger one nodded and gestured to the other. But they didn't go far.

"Not my idea," she told Tully, her eyes darting back to the men to indicate it was them she was talking about.

"From what I understand, your husband simply took your houseboat out for a ride. Your husband and your children – two, right?"

She nodded and Tully could immediately see just the mention of the kids caused a reaction. There was a shift in her posture, her shoulders actually slumped forward if only for a moment or two, as though she had been carrying a heavy weight and just remembered it was still there. Her eye contact had been piercing but now there was a flicker in the brilliant blue that betrayed the fatigue, maybe even a hint of panic.

"George builds boats for a living. He built our houseboat. And he can certainly handle it on stormy waters."

"This was supposed to be a family outing?"

"Yes. I was meeting them but I got delayed." Her eyes slipped past Tully and past the parking lot toward the emerald green water of the Gulf.

Tully studied her face, thought he saw regret. He could tell it wasn't the first time she had been late for a family outing. Maybe her husband was driving home that point. Teaching her a lesson. Tully's ex-wife used to work late all the time. She'd cancel out on him and his daughter Emma constantly, so much so that after the divorce he and Emma hardly missed her at all.

Pensacola Beach had quieted in the time since Tully and Maggie arrived. A few tourists were still out on the beach. Despite the red flag, a couple of daredevil surfers were riding the waves. Others had gone indoors. Tully could see a full deck at the restaurant, Crabs. The dark sky had even set off the parking lot lights.

For as much as the senator appeared in a hurry, now she seemed contemplative, still watching the gulf as if she hoped to see the houseboat crest over the next set of waves. Tully couldn't imagine George Ramos taking his kids out with a monster storm coming even if he thought he could teach his senator wife a lesson. But then Tully had seen people do a lot of strange things to each other. Still, he knew when to keep his mouth shut. She must have suspected what he was thinking.

"I know something's terribly wrong," she said.

Finally she looked at Tully, met his gaze. There was a firm resolve in her eyes but he caught a glint of sadness before she could stow it away.

"And they wouldn't have left without me."

CHAPTER 4

BY MAGGIE'S CALCULATIONS Liz Bailey had been down on the houseboat for nine minutes. Shouldn't that be enough time to know if anyone was aboard? If there were injuries? Whether or not they needed to send down the rescue basket or the medevac board?

"Have you seen her yet?" Wilson asked Kesnick for the third time.

"Nothing yet."

"Where the hell's that cutter?"

"They said less than an hour," Tommy Ellis told him.

Wilson shook his head in exaggerated frustration. But Maggie understood. An hour seemed like forever.

To make matters worse, the rain had started. Not a few raindrops or a light shower but a torrential downpour. The helicopter rocked and jerked despite Wilson's best efforts. Maggie's heart thump-thumped against her ribcage with the rhythm of the rotors. Sweat trickled down her back. The helmet threatened to suffocate her. She pushed back the visor. It didn't help.

Fortunately, she was too concerned about Bailey to pay attention to the churning in her stomach. Each jolt of the helicopter sent new spasms of nausea. She tasted blood before she realized she was biting down on her lower lip.

"Is she still with us?" Wilson wanted to know.

Kesnick pulled on the cable till it was taut. He had slowly let out sections, a little at a time as Bailey moved from the top deck to the bottom and then as she disappeared inside. Now he nodded to Wilson when he seemed convinced that she was still attached.

"Give her a tug."

"I have already."

"Visibility is turning to crap," Tommy Ellis said. "Pretty soon we won't be able to see her."

"We can't be out here much longer," Wilson told them. "I'm gonna take us down closer. Kesnick keep an eye out."

Maggie white-knuckled the straps on the side of the helicopter. Wilson's attempt to lower the craft met resistance. The wind gusts grabbed them, rocking and swaying every inch. Then suddenly they dropped. A freefall.

"Son of a bitch." Wilson wrestled them back from a roller coaster plunge.

Maggie's holstered revolver dug into her side and she realized how totally defenseless she felt. The void of control overwhelmed her. It wasn't motion sickness. It was the inability to do anything but sit back.

"I see her," Kesnick yelled as he slid his visor up for a better look. "She's waving from the lower deck."

"What does she need?"

Maggie watched Kesnick's face. Tanned and weathered. Crinkle lines at the eyes. Not an easy read. The man kept his expressions intact but this time she saw his eyes go wide.

"She's telling us to back away."

"What the hell?"

Maggie scooted along the side of the cabin as far as her seat belt would allow. She craned her neck and she could see Bailey leaning over the railing. Her right arm was raised with an open palm like she was waving at them but instead she pumped her hand back and forth.

Just as suddenly as the downpour began, it lightened. Even the helicopter steadied to a sway. Bailey could be seen more clearly and there was no mistaking her meticulous, slow but persistent hand signals.

"Do you see anyone else?" Wilson asked.

Kesnick shifted and twisted. So did Maggie.

"Could be someone inside. But I don't see anybody."

And Bailey didn't give anything away. If someone was threatening her and telling her to send her flight crew away, she wasn't looking to him.

"Maybe there's something on board," Kesnick said. "Explosives?"

"Then she needs to get her ass back up here. Now. Pull her up."

Maggie noticed a new hand signal just as Kesnick grabbed at the cable. He noticed, too, and stopped.

"Wait. There's more."

Bailey was grasping her clenched fist then pulling and separating.

"She's disconnecting from the hoist hook," Kesnick said and Maggie heard the panic in his voice.

"Son of a bitch." Wilson yelled. "Don't let her do it, Kesnick. Pull her ass up. Get her the hell out of there."

Kesnick scrambled to get his feet set. Then he double-fisted the cable, but Maggie could see it was too late. Bailey had already disconnected and the cable spun free.

Kesnick fell backwards. "Damn it!"

Wilson and Ellis both twisted around in their seats, but they wouldn't be able to see out the cabin window or door from their seats at the controls. Still, Maggie saw the stunned looks on their faces.

Kesnick scooted back into position.

"She's pushing us off again," he told the others.

Then Maggie saw Bailey raise her arm straight up, open palm facing forward.

"She's signaling that she's alright," Kesnick translated.

Bailey's arm stayed up.

"Maybe she just wants us to get out of the weather," Tommy Ellis said.

Maggie didn't think he sounded convincing though the storm was beginning to intensify again.

The wind gusted and sent the helicopter rocking. Another layer of dark clouds rolled in over them, this time flickering with streaks of lightning. Thunder rumbled and Maggie could feel its vibration against her back.

"Yeah, we've got to head back before we get knocked out of the sky."

"You can't just leave her," Maggie said.

The men went quiet. It was her first sentence since they had left the beach. Kesnick concentrated on Bailey whose arm was still raised.

"You know the rules, O'Dell. None of us are allowed to deploy except the rescue swimmer."

Yes, she did remember Wilson telling her that the last time.

"My job is to make sure the family on that houseboat returns safely to shore," she told them.

"A cutter's on its way," Ellis repeated.

"Something's wrong." It was Kesnick.

Maggie turned to look back down at Bailey. Her right arm was still raised but now she was waving it from side to side, a brisk, forceful wave.

"What is she telling us?" Maggie demanded when Kesnick failed to relay the message. "What does that mean?"

"Emergency," Kesnick said. "Needs assistance." He turned to Wilson. "She's in trouble."

"I'm going down." Maggie had already unhooked her seat belt and was sliding over to Kesnick.

"Like hell you are." But Wilson was struggling to keep the helicopter steady. Rain lashed at the sides.

Kesnick started preparing the cable. Maggie had done this before but somehow that didn't make it easier. She relied on adrenaline to push her toward the cabin door.

"You have no authority, O'Dell. This is my aircraft."

"You have no authority over me, Commander Wilson. That boat down there is the only reason I'm here. And something's going on whether we can see it or not."

"No one deploys except the rescue swimmer. Those are the rules, O'Dell."

"I've never been very good at following rules."

Maggie yanked off her helmet to end any further discussion. Without the helmet and ICS, she wouldn't be able to hear Wilson. It didn't stop him from yelling at her. But Kesnick was already helping her. He handed her a Seda lightweight helmet, just like the one Bailey wore. Maggie pulled it on and didn't bother to tuck her hair up into it.

Kesnick reached around her, looping and securing the harness. He positioned the quick strop over her shoulders, showing her – reminding her – how to work it and where to hold on. She snapped the goggles into place. Then she tested her gloved hands on the cable and realized she must be completely out of her mind.

She looked directly into Kesnick's eyes and saw his intensity. He leaned into her and yelled, "Let me do all the heavy lifting. You just hang on. I'll get you down."

But they both knew she wouldn't be coming back up.

He tapped her on the chest, two fingers right below her collarbone, just like he had with Bailey. The universal signal for "ready." She gave him a thumbs up and slid herself out of the helicopter door.

Almost immediately Maggie went into a spin, a dizzy, wild ride. She tucked her chin and dug her heels together so the cable wouldn't wrap around her neck. The wind was heartless and only accelerated the spinning. Rain pelted her. The thump-thump of the rotors continued to compete with her heart. Thunder roared above. Or at least she thought it was thunder. It was difficult to distinguish.

Her goggles clouded with the spray of rain. It didn't matter. She had her eyes squeezed tight. She knew if she opened them it would only add to the dizziness. She waited for the spinning to stop but even as Kesnick lowered her, it continued.

After what seemed like an eternity, her heels connected with something more solid than air. Maggie opened her eyes. Through the blur of her goggles she saw the upper deck of the houseboat. She pushed off and swung herself to the lower deck, sliding past the railing.

She felt Bailey's hands before she really saw the woman. Bailey pulled her down and helped disconnect her. She seemed in a hurry. The noise of the helicopter, the storm and the waves hitting the boat filled Maggie's ears and even when Bailey's mouth moved, Maggie couldn't make out the words. But she looked worried and frantic.

Maggie yanked the goggles down in time to see the cable – their only connection to the outside world – zip back up to the helicopter. Bailey was gesturing to them. The same signals, one after another. Telling them to back away, followed by "I'm alright" then immediately contradicting herself with the signal for "emergency, in trouble."

Maggie tried to understand, tried to catch Bailey's eyes. As she glanced away for an answer she suddenly saw a man underneath the deck's awning, hidden from view of the helicopter. He was on the far end of the houseboat but Maggie could still see what he held on his shoulder. Even in the blur of wind and rain she knew exactly what it was. He was aiming an RPG right at the helicopter.

CHAPTER 5

TULLY CHECKED HIS MESSAGES. He had texted Sheriff Langley about Maggie's Coast Guard crew. Surely there had been some word radioed in from them. But the latest response from the sheriff was annoyingly short: NOTHING.

How could there be nothing? That was bullshit!

Tully waited in his rental. He sat facing the Gulf, shifting his eyes from the black rolling mass of clouds that flickered with electricity to watching in his rearview mirror as the senator talked to her personal men-in-black. The clouds had turned day into night.

He tried calling Sheriff Langley for a second time, but the call went directly to voice mail. The sheriff would be pissed if he discovered Senator Delanor Ramos had passed on even a courtesy meeting with him. Was he pissed enough to withhold information? And why didn't she understand this? Wouldn't she want every possible law enforcement officer working to help? Or was it more important to keep the truth from getting out? Everything was political, either an asset or liability. Was the truth a liability in this case?

Something had obviously happened to her family. Maybe their houseboat simply broke down along with the radio. Could that happen with a half-million dollar boat? But she didn't believe it was that simple. She'd said as much.

He ran a hand through his hair. Now he could see the sheet of white under the clouds. In minutes that sheet of rain would be on top of them. He sent another text to Maggie. None had been answered. He didn't expect this one to be either, but he had to keep trying.

The passenger door opened and Senator Delanor Ramos hopped up and into the seat. She shoved an oversized tote onto the floormat beside her feet and buckled herself in, getting comfortable like she was going to spend an afternoon sightseeing. Tully craned his neck to see what her bodyguards were doing. If he wasn't mistaken, the black Escalade wasn't waiting on them.

She saw him looking in the rearview mirror and before he could ask, she said, "They would have only gotten in the way." Already she looked relieved.

And suddenly Tully realized that this was more serious than he thought. She was narrowing down her liabilities to just him. The fewer people who knew, the better.

What the hell was going on?

If his family were missing out at sea he would be calling in the cavalry, wanting all available personnel helping. Instead, the senator was counting on two FBI agents and one Coast Guard aircrew.

"You never answered my question," Tully said. "What exactly do you suspect has happened?"

"Agent Tully . . . Tully," she corrected herself even as she lightened her tone. After all, she was stuck with only him. "If I knew what happened to my family I wouldn't need the FBI, would I?"

"You obviously have some idea or you'd simply let the Coast Guard handle it."

He glanced over, but her face was turned to the window.

"I fear there's nothing simple about this."

He noticed her hands. While the rest of her body looked calm and under control, the fingers of her right hand twisted and turned her wedding ring, tugging it up over her knuckle only to shove it back down and start again.

CHAPTER 6

MAGGIE RIPPED AT THE FLIGHT SUIT'S zipper. Without being told, she knew the man with the rocket launcher on his shoulder was not the only terrorist on board. She needed to disarm herself before they did it for her. Bailey immediately saw what Maggie was doing and moved her body, but she wasn't just trying to block Maggie from the view of the man on deck. Bailey was also trying to stand in front of the window.

So someone else was there, watching. Of course, they were.

They'd needed to stay out of sight until the helicopter left. And Bailey's hand signals were supposed to accomplish that. No wonder the woman was so determined to get them to back off. The choice presented to her must have been to make the helicopter disappear or they would do it with a rocket. But they weren't versed in Coast Guard hand signals. They had no idea that while Bailey had told her aircrew to back off and that all was fine, she had also told them there was an emergency and that she was in trouble.

Maggie caught Bailey's eyes. They darted toward the boat and the window behind her. Then she blinked once, twice, three times. So there were three of them.

Maggie glanced over Bailey's shoulder to the man with the rocket then back at Bailey. She didn't know how to ask if he was included in the three. Before she could figure it out, Bailey gave a slight nod. Then her eyes darted down to the deck floor at Maggie's feet.

It looked like an oversized tackle box attached to the deck with metal brackets. A bungee cord kept it shut. Maggie tucked her hands inside of her flight suit though she had unzipped it to her waist. Her fingers tugged her shoulder holster free but like her hands, she held it hidden inside the suit.

When the next set of waves crashed up over the deck, the boat tipped and Maggie went down to her knees, pretending to lose her balance. Bailey teetered in front of her, arms outstretched as she grabbed the railing on one side and the wall with the other. She provided the perfect barricade.

Maggie grabbed at the bungee cord. She pulled up and slid the holster with the revolver into the tackle box in one quick motion, letting it slam shut. There was no relief watching her only control, her only hope of defense, disappear out of sight. Before she stood back up another wave knocked her back to her knees. She looked up at Bailey and saw the young woman's eyes trying to get her attention as she tapped her chest. When Maggie didn't understand, Bailey pricked at the emblem on her dive suit and pointed with her chin at Maggie then at the tackle box.

Her FBI badge. Of course. Bailey wanted her to dump it in the box. Maggie's fingers fished back into her flight suit, found the wallet and shoved it in under the lid.

The thunderclouds had been roaring overhead with lightning streaks that seemed to crackle. Waves swished and rain pelted the aluminum sides of the boat making it sound like a tin can being used as target practice for an AK-47. But the sound that drew Maggie's attention and sent her pulse into a panic was the helicopter leaving. The sound of the rotor wash lifted. The engine noise reduced to a hum, fading fast. And then it was swallowed up in the reverberation of the storm.

Their lifeline. *Gone.*

CHAPTER 7

TULLY TRIED TO PAY ATTENTION TO the street signs – at least the ones he could make out through the downpour – even though he followed Senator Delanor Ramos' directions. They had gone over two long bridges in blinding rain while the water churned below. Traffic had slowed down to twenty miles per hour. Tully tight-fisted the SUV's steering wheel, fighting against the wind gusts. They were on Scenic Highway now, a long winding two-lane that ran parallel to one of the bays.

"This associate," Tully said, "we couldn't just call him?" He had to raise his voice over the accelerated squeak-and-slash of the windshield wipers. The rain pelted the vehicle's roof.

"I tried. It went directly to voice mail."

In the streetlights and headlights Tully could see water rushing over the highway. Red taillights winked up ahead and he pumped the brakes slowly to avoid locking them up. It looked like there were broken branches covering one lane of traffic. Huge live oaks grew on the bluffs, the area between the highway and the water. Branches overhung the road in places.

"Tell me about this business associate," Tully said. He felt like he was yelling over the pounding of rain.

"They used to be partners."

"Building boats?"

"Yes. But Ricardo isn't a builder. Or a designer. I doubt that he could build a doghouse."

She was wringing her hands again. Glanced at her wristwatch and checked her cell phone. Just the reminder of Ricardo's incompetence – or maybe it was only the debris in the road – seemed to make her restless.

He could tell she was trying to decide how much to tell him.

"He helped with the financing." Another pause. "Building boats is expensive – materials, labor. Sometimes clients pay at different stages of completion. Sometimes they pay upon delivery."

There was something about the way she talked about her husband's business, and not just Ricardo, that made Tully realize she didn't approve.

"So Ricardo is rich?" he asked.

The senator burst out laughing. She had to wipe tears from her eyes and shook her head as if it was the most ridiculous thing she had heard.

"No," she finally managed. "Ricardo is not rich. He's a big talker. He missed his calling. Ricardo should have been a politician."

"You don't sound like you approved of their partnership."

"No, I didn't. They grew up together in the slums of Bogota. Ricardo's not even family but George is constantly looking after him. Bailing him out. Whenever there's trouble I know where to look because it usually has something to do with Ricardo."

It was their turn to use the single lane and Tully eased the SUV around the debris. The branch had taken some electrical lines with it. Water was running across the highway, almost to the chassis of the sedan in front of him. He was grateful he'd insisted on an SUV. Still, it was crazy to be out visiting old partners. He wanted to be back at the air station waiting for word on Maggie and her crew. Maybe they had already found the houseboat. How far out could a boat like that go in weather like this?

"How much farther is it?" he asked her, not bothering to keep his impatience from his voice.

"Not far. About another mile and then a left on Creighton. It's just a few blocks up from there."

The bungalow set back from the street. The detached garage was obviously added, almost as large as the house. Up and down the street Tully could see house lights on, families staying inside and taking shelter from the storm. The storm drains couldn't keep up with the rain that still came down in sheets. Water gushed over the curbs, flooding lawns and driveways.

Tully pulled the SUV as close to the house as possible but there was already a Jeep parked in front of the garage. It would still be a jog to the front door. By the time he got under the small awning he'd be drenched. Senator Delanor Ramos must have been thinking the same thing. She was pulling out an umbrella from her tote bag. When she reached for the door handle he realized she expected to go with him.

"Wait. Why don't you stay here? I'll see if he's even home."

She looked back at the house and seemed to consider this. Electrical lines danced above and tree branches creaked. Tully could see a faint light behind the tightly drawn blinds. But that was it.

He didn't wait for a response. He wanted to get this over with. He opened the SUV's door and leaped out, slamming the door as he took off in a sprint. The water ran ankle deep in places, covering the front lawn. If there was a sidewalk, Tully couldn't see it.

Thunder rumbled overhead and in the flashes of lightning he thought he saw someone standing in the trees alongside the house. It was enough for him to grab inside his Windbreaker for his Glock. But when he finally made it under the front door's awning he couldn't see anyone.

Was the wind and rain playing tricks on his eyesight? He wiped a hand over his face and his head swiveled around, trying to take in the yard and street and the narrow passage between the house and garage.

But there was no one. No pedestrians, no cars. Not even farther up the street.

Tully knocked on the door just as the thunder clashed. He waited and knocked again, harder. He tried the doorknob and to his surprise it turned. He eased the door open with one hand and gripped his weapon in the other.

"Hello? Mr. Ricardo?"

He noticed the flies first. Swarms of them in the faint light of table lamp. Then he noticed the smell.

Tully slowly entered. His eyes darted everywhere as he took small steps, his weapon drawn and leading. He didn't need to go far when he saw the living room's back wall. Warm sunshine yellow sprayed and splattered with blood.

"Oh my God."

He heard the senator behind him in the doorway. Tully threw out his left hand.

"Stay back," he warned as he continued farther inside. Right around the wide archway door he found the body slumped against the refrigerator. The man was in his underwear. His right kneecap was blown away as were several of his fingers. But the deathblow was a single shot to the forehead.

It looked like Ricardo hadn't been able to talk his way out of this one

CHAPTER 8

THE MAN WITH THE RPG was named Diego.
The one on the other side of the window with the
AK-47 was Felipe. Not that they formally intro-
duced themselves to Maggie and Liz. They spoke
Spanish to each other but surprisingly good Eng-
lish to their hostages. The fact that they were comfortable using each other's name in front of them,
kicked Maggie's heartbeat up a notch. They didn't
mind Maggie and Liz knowing because they
didn't expect their two intruders to tell anyone . . .
ever.

Now that the helicopter was gone the two men
had forced Maggie and Liz inside the boat. Liz's dive suit left little room for concealing weapons. Immediately the smaller of the two, Felipe, unzipped
Maggie's flight suit and raced his hands over her
body. She fought her basic instinct to punch away.
Thankfully he was in a hurry so his fingers poked
and prodded with little attempt at being salacious.

It was a relief of sorts just to get out of the
storm. Her hair was dripping, her adrenaline still
racing. Her nerves left raw from spinning on the cable ride down. She made herself take deep breaths
to steady herself, but the air inside smelled stale.
Stale with a metallic tang and the hint of cordite.
They had obviously interrupted something.

The dark paneled walls muffled the thunder
and rain to a battering but there was nothing to shut
off the sway. The boat was large enough that when

the waves pushed and shoved, the boat didn't jerk. It rolled, tipping and tilting one way until it threatened to send everything and everyone sliding. Then slowly it crested over a swell, heaved a sigh and began tipping in the other direction.

Diego had exchanged his RPG for an automatic handgun. Maggie felt it in the small of her back as he prodded her forward, at times almost pushing her into Liz. Felipe led them through the narrow hallway. Polished cherry wood rose from floor to ceiling broken up only by the living room's bookcases and bar, and the kitchen's stainless-steel appliances and granite countertops. No cost had been spared. And although glassware rattled and wine bottles clinked against each other, everything appeared to be staying in place despite the motion.

As they passed closed doors Maggie tried to listen for sounds of life. They were told there were six on board including the senator's teenaged daughter, her eight-year old son and her husband. If this was an abduction, they had to be here somewhere. Hopefully unharmed.

Perhaps Felipe read her mind. At the next door he stopped. He grinned back at Diego and said something Maggie didn't understand. Their Spanish was different somehow. Not what she was used to.

Diego laughed and Felipe pushed the door open, making sure it swung wide enough for them to see inside. He gestured for Liz to take a look but he was showing off, not asking for them to go into the room. Maggie saw Liz's shoulders drop but she managed to mask her emotions.

Then it was time for Maggie's sneak peek. And Felipe was anxious, the grin never leaving his face.

Inside the laundry room three bodies were sprawled out on top of each other, purposely stacked to accommodate the small space. At the top of the heap, a woman laid with her back arched, flopped over the other two. Her head and shoulders faced the doorway, only she stared wide-eyed at them from upside down. The bullet hole in her forehead still oozed.

So here was the crew. And Maggie understood clearly what Felipe was telling her and Liz. He wasn't just showing off their handiwork. He was telling Maggie and Liz that they would soon be joining the pile.

CHAPTER 9

TULLY HAD INSTRUCTED THE SENATOR to go back and stay in the SUV. To his surprise, she had obeyed without argument or discussion. Despite how tough the woman was, he knew the scene inside Ricardo's house was not something she had ever experienced before. And although she had been withholding information and dealing it out piecemeal to Tully since the minute they met, he also knew, that she had not expected or even suspected this.

The most frustrating part for Tully? Not fifteen minutes after finding Ricardo, the senator's political instinct already started kicking into gear. As soon as Tully jumped back into the SUV she was insisting they leave.

"A patrol unit is on the way," Tully explained.

"I can't be here when they arrive."

He looked over at her but she was staring ahead through the blurred windshield. The streetlights cast her face in shadow.

"Are you suggesting I leave the scene?"

"You've reported it, correct? It's not like we can tell them anything."

Which wasn't entirely true. He knew there was plenty the senator could tell the local law enforcement about Ricardo that they might never know.

"I've already called Raymond." And she said this as though she was pulling rank on him. "He understands the situation. He told me he'd take care of things."

Tully saw that she had her cell phone clutched tightly in her hand. The faceplate was still lit. For a woman who was careful and deliberate about her every move and concerned about her actions recorded and accounted for, he knew that her call to the FBI assistant director had been an added risk.

"Where do you suggest we go from here?"

"Back to the beach."

"Another business associate?"

"No," she said, but she winced as though his sarcasm had struck a nerve. "A friend."

It took them forever to backtrack. More branches were down. The water rushed across streets and in places so high that it looked as if it swallowed the tires of small sedans. Many were stranded along the sides. But it didn't seem to stop people from venturing out. There was still a remarkable amount of traffic.

Once they crossed the bridge and were back on the beach, the senator pointed to a marina on the gulf side.

"I'm hoping Howard will have something more to tell us."

"Howard is the friend?"

She nodded.

"Yours or your husband's?"

"Both. But he knows George. He's known him for a very long time."

"Like Ricardo?"

"No, not like Ricardo. Not at all like Ricardo." She shook her head as if she was trying to forget the image. "Howard is a friend. And we keep our houseboat here."

"So Howard may have seen them leave?"

"Howard would never let George take a boat out in weather like this, especially with the kids."

"Would he have stopped George?"

She seemed to consider this for a beat too long then said, "I doubt it. When George puts his mind to something there usually is no further discussion."

Tully pulled up as close as he could to the shop. The rain continued, drumming down and interspersed with wind gusts that sent the rain horizontal in violent blasts. Thunder shook the vehicle. Lightning streaked through the sky tinting the world a neon blue and crackling like electrical sparks.

The two-story shop had a marlin painted on the side and orange and blue letters that read: Howard Johnson's Deep-Sea Fishing. Beside it was Bobbye's Oyster Bar. Both looked closed though there was a faint light on in the shop.

Bistro tables were shoved against the bar's south wall. Chairs were turned over and stacked securely on top of the tables then chained down. Still, the wind rattled the cast iron. Across the boardwalk boats of all sizes rocked in their slips and lurched against their tie-down lines.

Though she still had the umbrella in her hand Senator Delanor Ramos made no attempt to open it. They were both soaking wet. Still, she carried it as she ran for cover under the shop's awning. A graceful run, almost a prance – Ginger Rogers in three-inch heels. Tully followed, his size thirteen's finding puddles already deep enough to swallow his loafers. Gwen would kill him. She had bought him the Italian leather shoes for one of their anniversaries.

How awful was it that he couldn't remember which anniversary? And then, even through the crashes of thunder, without his mind missing a beat, he immediately thought – how awful was it that your significant other bought you shoes for an anniversary? It was a crazy thing to think about on a night like this one. But it was a crazy night.

To his surprise the shop door opened despite the CLOSED sign in the window. A huge man stood behind the counter, towering over it. Barreled chested with muscular arms. He wore a bright colored boat shirt and white linen trousers. His thick hair was completely white as was his mustache and wide sideburns, although he didn't look older than sixty.

The only light in the shop came from inside the display cases and a neon sign – another marlin – this one, brilliant green and yellow. The neon danced in the reflection of the glass cases. Along with the lightning, it cast the entire shop in an otherworld illumination. Tully couldn't help thinking the man looked more like a captain of a spaceship rather than a deep-sea fishing boat.

"Can I help you folks?" he asked before he looked up. The baritone voice was kind and gentle despite the fact that he already had closed for the day. When he did look up, he had to do a double take. As soon as he recognized the senator he smiled – bright white teeth and laugh lines – and he shook his head. "Ellie, what in the world are you doing out in weather like this?"

He didn't wait for her reply. He came around the counter and engulfed her in a hug.

The tough-as-nails powerbroker of a senator, hugged him tight, standing on tiptoes to do it, and when he let her go, Tully saw her swat tears from her eyes.

"Howard, it's good to see you."

"I saw the boat was gone," he said before the question was asked. "What is George up to this time?"

CHAPTER 10

"JORGE, HERE ARE THE VISITORS," Felipe called out.

Diego had stayed back at the laundry room while Felipe had shoved Maggie and Liz forward onto a deck that was glassed in and protected from the storm. Even in the dark Maggie could see the waves crashing up and over the outside railings. She recognized it as the steering cabin of the boat.

A dark-haired man sat in the captain chair behind the steering wheel and in front of a panel of instruments. He glanced over his shoulder but only briefly. His attention stayed focused on the instruments that were barely lit.

Maggie had felt the engine come to life as they were walking through the narrow hallway. The vibration had rumbled under their feet and she knew the boat was moving again. She tried to remember what Tommy Ellis had said about the Coast Guard cutter. It was less than an hour away. How long ago was that? If the houseboat started moving in the opposite direction would the cutter ever find it? She wanted to ask Liz. She tried to read the younger woman's expression now that she was able to see her face.

Felipe motioned for them to sit on one of the benches alongside the wall. When Maggie didn't comply quickly enough he shoved her down. The man behind the steering wheel turned and scowled at him.

"Really, Felipe?"

"What? They are federales."

"Yes, and if you kill one of them this will be the end."

From Maggie's angle she could see Diego. He was dragging one of the bodies from the laundry room out onto to the deck. Somehow he worked the rocking of the boat and wind to his advantage. Instead of struggling, he waited for the tilt then raised the body up and let the wind and waves push it over the railing.

Maggie looked away, biting back the anger and helplessness she was feeling. Her mind tried to work the pieces together. Initially when she saw the RPG she thought terrorists had pirated the boat. It made sense. Senator Delanor Ramos was a powerful and outspoken political official. But political motivation seemed to drift away the more she watched the two thugs. Though perhaps Jorge was their mastermind.

Revenge or kidnapping seemed more likely. The houseboat was clearly luxurious. She had no idea of the senator's financial situation but a ransom would fit the profile of men like Diego and Felipe.

Then into this macabre nightmare a little boy wandered in from a doorway at the opposite end. He was dressed in baggy shorts and an Angry Birds T-shirt. He ignored the rest of them and ran to the man at the helm.

"Daddy, Angelica is hogging the X-box."

The man patted the boy and pulled him up onto his lap. Maggie exchanged a stunned look with Liz. She couldn't believe it. Jorge was George Ramos.

CHAPTER 11

TULLY FIDGETED WHILE HOWARD pulled out an expensive looking bottle of liquor. He set three crystal-cut rocks glasses on a bistro table in the corner of the shop. As Tully wandered over he noticed the shelf that ran a foot below the high ceiling. It lined all four walls and displayed miniature model boats, tightly packed, end-to-end. They were the type that someone painstakingly had put together and painted, delicate lines and tiny pieces. He couldn't help glancing at Howard's large hands. They looked more like they belonged to a boxer than a man who applied fine details to tiny bits of plastic.

The senator had just told Howard about Ricardo. Tully couldn't help noticing that he didn't look shocked, not even surprised. Those big hands were steady and graceful as he poured the amber liquid. He slid a glass in front of the senator then set down a second one for Tully before he filled his own glass.

"Some of the old dogs have come sniffing around again in the last couple of years." He told the senator as he glanced from her to Tully then back.

"Oh, it's okay, Howard. He's one of Raymond's agents." Then to Tully she explained, "Howard and George used to . . . how do I put this?" She looked to Howard for help.

"We had some interesting friends." He took a sip of the liquor. To the senator he said, "If these old acquaintances have been coming around to me, they might be bothering George, too."

"He hasn't said anything." She caught herself and added, "But of course, he wouldn't say anything to me."

Tully rolled his eyes. She had been talking in carefully measured phrases all day. He wasn't going to sit here and listen to them water down the details and talk around the facts.

"So you and George ran drugs," Tully said bluntly and both of them stared at him as though he walked into a cocktail party naked. "Let me guess. A Columbian cartel."

Still, neither responded.

"Which means, probably cocaine, right?" Tully continued, pretending he knew the facts as he guessed.

Did they think he was stupid? The senator had been screwing with him all afternoon, doling out information ounce by ounce. That was fine until a dead guy showed up.

"No disrespect intended, Senator Delanor Ramos," he tamped down his impatience. "Whether you want to admit it or not, your husband is involved in something. And it looks like it's going to be messy for you politically."

She was staring at him. Her jaw clamped tight, her lipstick long gone. She had peeled out of her soaking-wet jacket but the rest of her clothing was also damp. Hair dripping and yet her hand dashed up to swipe back a disheveled strand. She didn't look any closer to budging on the truth.

Tully had never understood what he referred to as "the political class," and in the past he was grateful his dealings with them were far and few between. In Tully's opinion, they lived by an obscene creed that defied logic. A creed that raised ideologies and self-preservation above common sense. But his new boss, Assistant Director Raymond Kunze had carved out a career by doing favors or as Tully believed – by sucking up to select congressmen and senators. Tully and Maggie had spent over a year trying to function by Kunze's ridiculous criteria.

"Are you willing to sacrifice your children for your husband?" Tully asked. This seemed to get her attention even if it looked like anger. "Are you willing to sacrifice all of them for your political career?"

"You have no right to judge me."

"Ellie," Howard said, putting a hand over hers and making it disappear but with the gentlest of touches. "Agent Tully's trying to help. And he's right. This is serious." Then he looked up at Tully. "What would you like to know?"

"You and George. What was it? Twenty-five years ago? Thirty? Florida was a major trafficking route."

"It's starting to be, again," Howard said. "A couple of the cartels are reclaiming old trafficking channels. The Sinaloa and the Zetas are warring over the routes through Juarez and Tijuana. A tremendous amount of resources have been focused on the Mexican border." Howard shrugged. "Suddenly the Gulf of Mexico and the Florida coastline are looking very good once again."

"And your old cartel?" Tully asked.

"They're calling themselves Choque Azul now. Let's just say improvisation was always one of their greatest assets. Did you see in the news, somewhere off the coast of Columbia a submarine was found?"

"Yeah, I remember reading something about that."

"The U.S. military almost immediately suspected the Russians. Maybe Chavez." Howard shook his head and smiled. "I'm pretty certain it was my old cartel. They've been looking for new vessels, new transports. Three or four months ago DEA confiscated a fishing boat off the shore of Puerto Rico. Nine hundred and twenty-five pounds of cocaine was seized. They found the bags under a boatload of mahi-mahi. That doesn't stop them. It's big business.

"A kilo of cocaine in the highlands of Columbia or Peru is worth about two-thousand dollars. In Mexico that same kilo goes to ten-thousand. Jump the border to the US and it's suddenly worth thirty-thousand. By the time it's broken down into grams to distribute for retail, that same kilos is now one-hundred thousand dollars.

"That much money involved, it's a whole lot easier to keep finding ways to fool the DEA and the Coast Guard than to battle the Zetas and Sinaloa. The Zetas." Howard stopped and studied Senator Delanor Ramos. "Well, you know from your congressional panels that it's nasty business these days."

But her eyes had wandered out to the storm. Her fingers of both hands wrapped around the glass, but Tully hadn't seen her take a sip.

"The Zetas," Howard continued. "A bunch of them got their start in this business as bodyguards for the Gulf cartels. Our bodyguards." He laughed.

"They're a bunch of thugs is what they are. Years ago people got in the way, they just disappeared. Used to be rumors that all the drug cartels had vats of lye. They were discreet about their kills. But this new bunch?"

He glanced at the senator again. She hadn't moved.

"They pride themselves," Howard said, "in using bloodshed to send their messages. Beheadings, dismemberment . . . anything to shock and awe not only to warn their enemies but the civilian populations in the areas where they hide in plain sight."

"Taking my family," Senator Delanor Ramos suddenly said. "Taking George and the houseboat. Do you suppose it's some sort of revenge or punishment for him not giving in to them?"

Tully wanted to ask why she thought George hadn't given in to them. But of course, he already knew why. He was her husband. However, it made perfect sense to Tully now that the situation might be quite the opposite. Not revenge. Not punishment. Was it possible that George Ramos was allowing his old drug cartel friends to use his houseboat?

He remembered the stories Howard was referring to. Tully had read about the speedboats coming into the Gulf and dumping crates and containers of drugs into the water. Then they bribed fishermen to pick them up. He hadn't thought about submarines. And actually it was a brilliant idea to use a family's houseboat. Even more brilliant in a storm like this?

The Coast Guard's response would be limited. If they did come across the houseboat their first concern would be that the family had gotten caught in the storm. A cutter would make sure they were returned safely, never suspecting that below deck there might be hundreds of pounds of cocaine stashed from a delivery in the middle of the Gulf.

That's when his cell phone finally rang. It startled him after being quiet all afternoon.

"R.J. Tully."

"Agent Tully, this is Commander Wilson." His voice sounded clipped and mechanical.

"You're back."

"Yes."

"I haven't heard from Agent O'Dell yet. How did it go?"

The Coast Guard pilot went silent.

"Commander Wilson?"

"Agent O'Dell didn't return with us."

CHAPTER 12

"**YOUR WIFE SENT US LOOKING** for you, Mr. Ramos," Maggie had told the man after his son had left the steering house.

George had sent the boy back to his cabin with the promise that he would buy him his own X-box to have all to himself. Before the boy left, George said, "Just don't tell your mom." And the boy grinned like it was a familiar game. Maggie wondered how many other things the boy wasn't supposed to tell his mother.

Now he said to Maggie, "Ellie worries too much." Then to Felipe he said, "She worries about everything. What people think of her. What they say about her."

Felipe wasn't interested. Instead, he pointed to something on one of the instrument panels. Maggie couldn't see from her seat on the bench. George nodded at him and calmly said, "Probably ten to twenty minutes at the most."

"Aren't you worried at all about your children?" Liz joined in.

"You want I should shut them up?" Felipe asked.

"No, it's okay. They don't have much time left."

The way he said it made Maggie break out in a cold sweat. Her pulse started to race and she checked her wristwatch. They had ten to twenty minutes before they ended up like the crew of this houseboat.

"To answer your question, my kids grew up on boats. This . . ." He gestured out at the storm and for the first time it appeared to be letting up. "This is a minor inconvenience because they can't be up on deck."

Maggie had thought – they had all believed – that George Ramos and his children had been abducted, their boat taken by force. These men certainly had a cache of serious weapons. A United States senator's husband and children would be a hefty ransom. Or it would exact a terrible blow of revenge. But George Ramos didn't look like he had his boat taken or commandeered by force. Instead, he appeared to be the one in charge.

"You're making a pick-up, aren't you?" Liz asked. "Is that what this is all about?"

That drew a smile from Felipe.

"You've got it all figured out," George said but he was focused on the panel of instruments again. He clicked buttons and twisted the steering wheel. Maggie could feel the vibration as the engine revved up a notch. They were going faster. And they were turning.

"You're meeting a drug boat," Liz said, not bothering to hide her anger. "That's why you're out here in the middle of a storm." She shook her head, disgusted.

Maggie looked over at her. The woman was a rescue swimmer but as part of the Coast Guard she was a trained guardsman. Was there any way they could overpower all three men? Diego and Felipe hadn't bothered to tie their hands or restrain them. Which only told Maggie that they would not hesitate at all to shoot them if they even dared to make a wrong move.

All she could think about was that her gun was clear on the other side of boat.

"How can you do this in front of your children?" Liz asked.

This time George Ramos looked at her but he was smiling and all he said was, "Fifteen more minutes."

Maggie thought about what Liz had said. But if they were meeting a drug boat why was he speeding up? She could hear the engine hum, almost a groan as it struggled to accelerate against the choppy water. Then all of a sudden the lights flickered. Not lightning but the electrical lights, even those on the instrument panel. Another flicker and everything went black.

"What the hell?"

Maggie grabbed Liz's wrist and pulled the woman to her feet. It took no more prodding than that. Both George and Felipe exchanged curses as Maggie and Liz were feeling their way back down the wood-paneled hallway.

CHAPTER 13

"WHAT DO YOU MEAN YOU left Agent O'Dell on the houseboat? How the hell did she get from your helicopter down onto the houseboat?"

"Oh, my God. They found the boat," Senator Delanor Ramos said when she overheard him. "Where are they? Are they okay?"

He waved her off. He was having a difficult enough time trying to hear what Wilson was telling him.

"A cutter is on its way," the commander explained. "We couldn't stay in the air or we'd be knocked out of the sky."

"You still didn't tell me how Agent O'Dell ended up on the boat."

"She left the helicopter without my consent. She disregarded my order."

Okay, Tully thought, so that did sound like Maggie, but only if she believed something serious was going down.

"What exactly do you think happened to the boat?"

"We couldn't see anyone on board. But RS Bailey was giving us mixed signals."

"What about George and the kids? Are they okay?" The senator grew impatient.

"Hold on, Commander," Tully said and to the senator, "They couldn't see anyone on board. A cutter's on its way."

"Oh, my God." Her fingers were back to twisting her wedding ring.

"Commander, won't it take forever in this storm for a cutter to find the houseboat?"

"They've been tracking it on radar ever since we gave them its position. Their turbo engines should put them on location any time now."

"Listen," Tully said, trying to figure out if anything he could tell the Coast Guard would even make a difference. "We have reason to believe members of a drug cartel took over the boat."

"Wait a minute, how do you know that? We haven't received anything."

Tully ignored the senator's pained look. "I have nothing official, okay? But you need to warn that cutter. There are most likely armed men aboard."

CHAPTER 14

MAGGIE THOUGHT SHE COULD hear another noise. Not a helicopter but a loud hum approaching. If Liz was right about them picking up a drug delivery then there was another boat close by. Right now all she could think about was getting through the pitch-black hallway. Liz stayed quiet. She kept her hand on Maggie shoulder and followed. She knew exactly where Maggie was headed.

They could already hear Felipe stumbling to find them back in the steering house. George wouldn't be able to leave as long as the boat's engine was engaged. Though she didn't know that for sure. Boat's probably had auto-pilot but could it be used in a storm?

Felipe was yelling to Diego in Spanish. And for a second Maggie worried that they might run right into the man. Had he finished flinging the dead crew members over the railing? Or was he back here in the laundry room retrieving the last one?

She held her breath, trying to listen. But she didn't slow down her pace. The engine still chugged and vibrated the floorboards. Certainly Diego would be cursing in the dark if he had been in the laundry room or even the hallway when the lights went out.

Her hip ran into a kitchen counter. She bit down on her lip but felt relief more than pain. If they'd made it to the kitchen they had passed the laundry room. The only window was further down, past the living room, past another hallway of floor to ceiling cherry wood paneling and bookcases. Not that windows mattered. It was too dark. Still, Maggie could see a flicker of lightning at the end of the tunnel.

"Two more doors," Liz whispered and Maggie realized that the rescue swimmer had counted them when they had been hostages.

At the other end of the hallway behind them she could hear Felipe slamming through the door from the steering house. It wouldn't take him any time at all to make his way through in the dark. Everything was bolted down. Maggie couldn't even shove anything in his path to slow him down.

Then the engine sputtered and went silent. George had turned it off. And now there were three men to worry about.

"Just on the other side of the next bookcase," Liz whispered again.

Maggie grabbed Liz's arm and exchanged places with her. If she had to, she knew she could take down Felipe, especially if he didn't see it coming. As if reading her mind, Liz kept hold of Maggie's wrist and pulled her along.

"It's right here," she said and the two of them patted down the wall looking for the door latch.

Liz found it first. The blast of wind and rain hit them in the face like buckshot. Maggie had to hold her breath. She tucked her chin and grab onto the railing. The tackle box would be close and yet Maggie couldn't see a foot in front of her.

Then she realized Liz was down on her hands and knees. She joined her.

"It's not here," Liz yelled.

"It has to be."

Lightning flashed and Maggie saw the box clamped down. She crawled closer. She could see the bungee cord that cinched the lid. A wave washed over the deck railing, knocking both of them into the wall. Maggie swiped a hand over her face and through the blur she thought she saw a light on the water. She pointed for Liz.

"Drug boat?"

Liz shook her head. "Bigger. I think it might be the cutter."

It was close. Minutes away. And yet, Maggie knew they might be dead in minutes.

She reached for the bungee cord and suddenly the deck lit up. A big man with a spotlight stood at the other end. Diego. He stood almost exactly in the same place where she had seen him with the RPG. This time he had the spotlight in one hand and an automatic rifle in the other.

Maggie continued to slide closer to the tackle box. Diego was shouting at them in Spanish. She grabbed the bungee cord and worked her hand under the lid. The box was deep. Where it had taken no time to toss her weapon down into it, it would take reaching her entire arm to find it. Before her fingers made purchase Felipe stormed out the same door.

He was angry. He was screaming at them but pointing and gesturing to Diego about the light that was approaching. Only now did Maggie realize that Liz had positioned herself, once again, in front of Maggie so that the men couldn't see. Maggie continued to slide her hand to the other side of the tackle box. Her arm was behind her and Felipe hadn't noticed quite yet. He still didn't suspect that they would have access to weapons. He thought they only wanted to escape.

Felipe gestured now for Diego to hurry while he waved the automatic handgun in Liz and Maggie's faces. He was speaking too quickly for Maggie to understand but she knew they would need to move Maggie and Liz to the other side of the boat, away from the approaching light so they could shoot them and throw them overboard.

Why couldn't she find her gun?

That's when George Ramos came out the door. He stood between them – Diego and Felipe on one side, legs spread and balancing themselves like experts in the wind and rain. On the other side was Liz and Maggie still on their knees. George looked to Maggie and held something up, waving it around above his head. In the glare of the spotlight she thought it looked like a gun.

"Is this what you're looking for, Agent O'Dell?"

Her service revolver. And she felt her stomach drop.

George Ramos brought the gun down. His arm stretched out. He fired two shots, expertly hitting both of his targets. The first caught Diego between the eyes. The second blast slammed into Felipe's right temple.

CHAPTER 15

THE RAIN HAD LET UP. Even the wind seemed to be giving them a break. But Tully saw lightning brighten the horizon just over the water. It would, indeed, be only a break. There was definitely more to come.

Moments ago the cutter had arrived with the houseboat named Electric Blue in tow. No one was allowed to board until given permission. Senator Delanor Ramos was not pleased but she waited.

When he saw Maggie he hardly recognized her. She still wore the orange flight suit. Her hair was a tangled mess. Her skin almost a sickly white. She and Liz Bailey stood shoulder to shoulder as the Coast Guard brass made them go through their ridiculous protocol.

Very little had been relayed back to them on shore, but they were told that George Ramos and his two children were safe and unharmed. Two men had, indeed, boarded the houseboat and attempted to take it over. Three members of Ramos's crew had been killed. And from what Tully understood, the two gunmen were also dead.

"I knew George would never put our children in danger," the senator said as she stood beside Tully.

They watched from inside the air station. Tully glanced over at her. Her tote bag in his rental SUV had provided her with a change of clothing. She had reapplied makeup and fixed her hair. The façade was back in place, everything back to normal. For her sake and for her kids, he hoped that was the case. After listening to Howard about drug cartels reclaiming old routes Tully didn't believe that this story was that easily explained away. If it were, George's "business associate," Ricardo wouldn't be dead. Tully was anxious to hear George's explanation.

On the pier, Maggie watched Liz. She was better at this than Maggie was. There would be reports to file and statements to sign. The Coast Guard and Homeland Security would make sure everything was properly handled. And at the same time, Maggie wanted to take Liz aside and ask, "What the hell happened out there?"

The cutter had taken on the houseboat within minutes of George Ramos shooting Diego and Felipe. When he pulled Maggie and Liz inside from the bloody deck he told them how relieved he was. That he had been frightened for his children. He handed them towels from the closest bathroom and offered them brandy. And the whole time Maggie noticed that he hadn't put down her revolver. He kept it in his hand like a reminder that he was still in charge. And it was in his hand when he stepped back out onto the lower deck, leaving them inside the cozy living room with the generator partially restoring electricity.

Maggie shouldn't have been surprised when George Ramos explained his story to the Coast Guard crew. Both she and Liz agreed that they didn't know what the situation was before they boarded. Drained and exhausted, Maggie realized that some things were not as they appeared. It wasn't impossible that a father would pretend to go along with a couple of madmen if he knew it would save his children.

George claimed the men had threatened him and were forcing him to meet their drug connection somewhere in the Gulf of Mexico. That scenario wasn't far from what Liz had suspected. He made his story sound so convincing that even Maggie found herself backtracking. She tried to remember pieces of dialogue. She still couldn't figure out how and when he had managed to get her gun out of the tackle box. Why had she been so sure that George was not only friends with Diego and Felipe, but that he was the one in charge?

"A man does whatever he needs to do to protect his children," George Ramos kept saying and twice he had said it while looking directly at Maggie and Liz.

Maggie wondered if the children would ever be questioned. She doubted it. Though she realized the children probably didn't know anything more than what their father had told them. They had been stashed away in their bedrooms playing video games.

As they exited the cutter she watched George with Angelica and Daniel as they met the senator on the pier. George scooped up Daniel and the family huddled together, exchanging hugs and kisses.

"It's the damnedest thing," Liz said, walking alongside Maggie.

Now that they were finally alone Maggie stopped and waited for Liz's eyes. It was breezy out in the middle of the pier but the rain was light and actually felt good. Behind them, crews were securing the cutter and the houseboat.

"Do you believe him?" she asked.

Liz glanced around. She nodded at someone and Maggie turned to see Tully making his way to them. Before Tully was in earshot, Liz answered, "Not in a million years."

"You're a sight for sore eyes," Tully said and surprised Maggie with a bear hug.

He patted Liz on the shoulder as she left them to rejoin her aircrew who were already yelling catcalls at her from the end of the pier.

"You okay?" he asked as they walked and followed in Liz's direction.

"I think I'll leave the helicopter rides to you in the future."

"That's a deal."

They were almost to the parking lot when Maggie noticed George Ramos heading back down the pier to his houseboat.

"What's he doing?" she asked Tully.

"Maybe he wants to get it to the marina and into its slip before the next bands of weather. It's an expensive boat."

She saw Senator Delanor Ramos and the two children getting into a black Escalade. Tully was probably right.

"Lots of holes in his story," Tully said as if reading her mind. "I doubt he's going to be asked to fill in any of those."

"Does his wife believe him?"

"I think she has to."

"Maybe I can ask him just one last question," Maggie said. She glanced over at Tully. "Care to come along?"

"I wouldn't miss it."

"Let the poor man board his boat first," she told him and they took up a leisurely pace.

George Ramos waved to the cutter's crew as he passed them on the pier. They were leaving as he went back to his boat. It had been a hell of night. Maggie could hear the men wishing him well. He didn't even notice Tully and Maggie as he climbed onto the lower deck of Electric Blue. He didn't look back as he entered the same side door where he had shot Diego and Felipe. All the blood had been washed away by the waves and the rain. The cutter crew hadn't been at all surprised when George explained how both men had fallen overboard when he shot them with her revolver.

But Liz and Maggie knew that the men hadn't fallen overboard. George had gone back out before the cutter arrived.

Maggie suspected he was lying about much more. Everyone presumed that the houseboat hadn't met up with the drug boat yet. That they were headed to pick up the delivery when Liz and Maggie interrupted. But what if they were wrong? What if they were on their way back?

Maggie gestured for Tully to climb aboard behind her. She opened the door gently, quietly and before she went inside she saw Tully had his weapon drawn. Hers was still being held by the Coast Guard.

With the dim lights, it was easy to follow the narrow hallway. She could hear George in one of the bedrooms down passed the kitchen. It sounded like he was moving furniture but Maggie knew that wasn't possible. Everything was bolted down. Before she got to the open bedroom door, she pressed her back against the paneled hallway wall and let Tully go around her.

She stayed in place and watched him step into the doorway. She watched Tully's face and immediately she knew that she was right.

Tully aimed his weapon and cleared his throat. "Stay right where you are, Mr. Ramos."

When Maggie looked in she couldn't believe it. The storage bins were pulled out from under the bed. A window bench was open exposing another storage area. All of them were stacked and packed with bags of cocaine.

George Ramos smiled and shook his head like he couldn't believe it.

"This is not what it looks like," he said.

"Choque Azul," Tully said suddenly. "I can't believe I missed it but my Spanish isn't so great." He glanced at Maggie but kept his Glock pointed on Ramos. "The drug cartel George used to work for. They call themselves Choque Azul now. Doesn't that mean Blue Shock?" Then to Ramos, he said, "You named your boat after them."

"Electric Blue," Maggie said. "This wasn't your first drug run."

"I can explain this." Ramos actually looked worried now.

"But we'll make sure it's your last," she added.

AUTHOR'S NOTE: *Electric Blue* was first published in 2012 and was one of three novellas in *Storm Season* with co-authors, J.T. Ellison and Erica Spindler.

AFTER
DARK

AFTER DARK

I-80 Heading West
Omaha, Nebraska

MADELINE KRAMER SLAMMED ON the brakes inches from the Lexus bumper in front of her.

"Calm down, Maty," she scolded herself and watched the Lexus driver give her the finger from out his window. She balled up her fist, disappointed that she wasn't able to return the gesture. She could have avoided rush hour traffic if she hadn't stopped by the office. Her first day of vacation was wasted and for what? Gilstadt wouldn't even look at her marketing proposal the entire time she was gone. And now she'd never make it to the cabin before dark.

She glanced in the rearview mirror. Why did she let the job take so much out of her? The lines under her eyes were becoming permanent. She raked her fingers through her hair, trying to remember the last time she had it trimmed. Were lines beginning to form at the corners of her mouth? How did she ever let herself get to this point?

A honking horn made her jump. She sat up and grasped the steering wheel in attention.

God, how she hated rush-hour traffic.

They were stopped again with no promise of movement. She glanced at her copy of the marketing proposal sitting in the seat beside her. Forty-two pages of research, staring up at her, mocking her. This was the hard copy, the stats and Arbitron ratings. What she left with Gilstadt included a five-minute video presentation. Six long days' worth of research and preparation, and Gilstadt had barely glanced at it, simply nodding for her to add it to one of the stacks on his desk. By the end of the day all her hard work would probably be buried under another stack.

Story of her life. Or at least, that's how it had been lately. Nothing seemed to be going right. One of the reasons she needed this vacation before she simply went mad.

Her cell phone blasted her back to reality. God, her nerves were shot. She let the phone ring three more times. Why hadn't she shut the damn thing off? Finally she ripped it from its holder.

"Madeline Kramer."

"Maty, hi, I'm glad I caught you."

Her entire body stiffened on impulse. "William, is everything okay? Where are you?"

"Everything's fine. Relax. I'm at home."

"I thought you left for Kansas City early this morning? Your conference."

"My presentation's not until later this week. Where are you? You're not at the cabin or you wouldn't have a cell phone connection."

"I stopped at the office."

"Jesus, Maty. It's your first day off. Are you still at the office?"

She clenched her fist around the steering wheel and tried to ignore the sudden tightness in the back of her neck.

"I'm almost at the cabin," she lied. "If fact, I may lose you soon. What is it that you need?"

"Need?"

"You called me," she reminded him. He was already distracted. She could hear something in the background. It sounded like a train whistle. Their home was no where close to train tracks. "You were glad you caught me," she tried again.

Why did he do this to her? He was checking up on her, again. She had come to resent his constant worry, his psychoanalysis, his treating her like one of his patients. Did he think he could try to talk her out of this one last time with more concerns that it might not be safe for her being out there all alone? No, she wasn't a camper. This wasn't about camping. This was about going some place to be completely away from everything and yes, everyone. Besides, she had listened to him enough to bring along her father's old Colt revolver. William didn't even know she had kept it from the estate sale. He hated guns. Hated the very idea of them being in the house.

"I just wanted to tell you I love you," he said.

Maty closed her eyes. Took a deep breath and moved the phone so he couldn't hear her releasing a long sigh. He did worry about her. He loved her. That was it. That was all. Her nerves were wound so tight she couldn't even see what she was doing to her marriage.

"I'm sorry, William. I love you, too."

"There might be thunderstorms tonight. I just wanted to tell you that. Oh and Maty, remember not to mix your meds with too much wine. Okay? I don't mean to be a nag but I saw that you packed several bottles."

Her face flushed. Embarrassment. A bit of anger. Calm. She needed to stay calm. He was concerned about her. That's all. Don't shove everyone out of your life, she told herself.

"Maty?"

"I'll remember."

"Promise?"

More and more of their conversations sounded like doctor and patient. No, that wasn't true. They sounded like parent and child.

"I promise, William."

"Good girl. Now you go out to your cabin retreat and get some rest. Relax, take it easy. I'll see you in three days."

Now if that didn't sound like a prescription. And patronizing.

Stop it!

She needed to stop sabotaging everything with her paranoia and her negative attitude. You get what you sow. That's what her mother always said. If you think good thoughts good things will come to you. The power of positive thinking. *What a bunch of crap.* Maty Kramer knew that everything she had gotten in life was because she had fought for it, not because she focused on positive thinking. Okay, so she hadn't been much of a fighter lately. Deep down the instinct must still exist, didn't it?

She found a hole in the traffic and gunned the engine. Traffic was moving again. She could relax, and yet a familiar throbbing began at the base of her neck and tightened the tension in her shoulders. It would take more than some peace and quiet to get rid of all this.

SHE TOOK HER EXIT OFF THE interstate and drove onto the two-lane highway that would take her far away from the city. She needed this vacation. She glanced at the marketing proposal. The shoulder pain eased its way down into her chest, following its regular path.

"God," she thought out loud, "I'm only thirty-five. A thirty-five year old woman shouldn't be having chest pains."

She pressed the button, sliding the window down and grabbed a handful of pages. She stretched her arm out the window and listened to the pages flapping in the wind, slapping each other and licking her wrist. She held her breath and told herself to let go. Just let go. Suddenly, she jerked her arm back into the car, holding the papers tightly in her lap.

"Am I going completely mad?"

She shook her head and placed the pages safely back on the seat, before she had time to reconsider.

IT WAS AFTER SEVEN WHEN SHE pulled up to the park office. The sun disappeared behind the massive cottonwoods and river maples. Maty had spoken to a woman in the park's office earlier in the day. She had assured Maty her late arrival wouldn't be a problem.

"I'll just leave your cabin key in an envelope and tape it to the door. You're in Owen, number two, dear. Remember that, because the key doesn't have any markings on it."

It sounded odd at the time, to leave something as valuable as a key on an office door for anyone to grab, but now looking at the place Maty understood. The small brick building sat in the middle of the woods, in the middle of nowhere. Shadows had already started to swallow what sunlight was left. One lonely lamppost glowed at the edge of the parking lot. There was a bare lightbulb above the office door. There were no other cars in the lot and no sign of anyone.

The woman had warned her. "It's the off-season, dear. You'll be the only one here. The park superintendent has a conference in Omaha. And I'm only here Friday through Monday. Are you sure you'll be okay, dear?"

"I'll be fine," she told the woman. It seemed even strangers didn't believe she could handle being on her own.

Now as she got out of the car she realized how good it felt to stretch and breath in the crisp, fresh air. Then she closed the car door and its thud echoed. There was something unsettling about the silence. A knot twisted inside her stomach. Was she prepared for all this quiet?

Of course, she was. It was late. She was hungry. She'd get to her cabin, slice some of the expensive cheeses she had splurged on, pour a glass of wine and before she knew it she would be relaxed and enjoying the beauty – and the quiet.

It really was quite lovely here. The trees had just begun to turn yellow and orange with some fiery red bushes in-between. Hidden in the treetops, locust whined and a whippoorwill called. A breeze sent fallen leaves skittering across the sidewalk in front of her.

As a kid she loved going to her grandfather's cabin in the woods. She used to go every year before, what her mother called, "grandpa's madness." The entire family would make a holiday of it, swimming in the lake, hiking in the woods and at night gathering around an open fire. Those were some of the best, happiest times of her life. If she could capture just a fraction of those feelings, this vacation would be a success.

But as she reached the office door Maty knew something wasn't right. She felt it almost as if someone had sneaked up behind her and tapped her on the shoulder. There was nothing on the door. The envelope with her cabin key was missing.

The woman simply forgot, Maty convinced herself. No one would take it. There was no reason to take an envelope with an unmarked cabin key. She told herself this as she hurried back to her car.

She could simply drive back to the city. Go home. But what would she tell William? It was exactly the kind of thing he would expect of her. And that was enough reason to not consider it.

Up the road and between the trees she noticed a light. What would it hurt to check it out? A sign at the end of a long driveway read Park Superintendent. The front door of the ranch-style house had been left open. Before Maty decided to stay or go a tall lanky man in a brown uniform appeared alongside her car. She jumped and accidentally tapped the car horn.

"You lost?"

Maty saw a patch on his sleeve that identified him as the Park Superintendent. He looked too young to be in charge of anything.

"No, I'm not lost," she said, rolling down her window, but only halfway. "I've rented one of your cabins for the week. I called the office earlier to let them know I'd be late. I'm afraid they forgot to leave my key for me."

"Helen never forgets. Maybe it just fell off the door."

Maty met him back at the office. They searched everywhere – in the bushes, under the bushes, in the grass. Darkness replaced shadows and Maty was getting impatient.

"Maybe Helen just forgot to put it on the door." He still wouldn't relinquish the fact that Helen just plain forgot.

"Or someone got to it before I did," Maty joked as she followed his tall shadow into the dark office.

"No, no that wouldn't be possible," he said in his deadpan tone, oblivious to her attempt at humor. "There's no one else here," he explained. "I'm getting ready to leave, too. Even the grounds men aren't due back until next week."

He flipped on the light switch in the office and both of them searched the peg board that held two keys for each cabin. Her eyes found Owen #2. Only one key was left.

Maty watched Ranger Rick, or whatever his name was, reach for the remaining key.

"See, I knew Helen must have gotten your key for you. It probably went home with her."

She didn't care anymore. She simply wanted to get to the cabin and get to bed.

"Sure, that's probably what happened."

By now it was dark despite a sky full of stars and a moon that was almost full. The park's trees grew thicker as she drove. Her car's headlights sliced through the darkness. She wondered, again, if this was a bad idea. Perhaps the lost key was a bad omen. She laughed out loud. Not even to her cabin, and already she was sabotaging her vacation.

THE CABINS WERE TUCKED BACK IN the woods, only patches of rooftop visible from the parking area. Small wooden signs and arrows indicated what path to follow for which cabin. She found the sign for Owen #2, slung her backpack over her shoulder and with a flashlight in one hand and grocery bag in the other, she followed the narrow trail. As she got closer she discovered the lake.

Maty stood paralyzed by the beauty of the moonlight on the water. A chill slid down her back. She shook her head and hugged the bag to her chest. It was a lake in the woods in the dark, and it was chilly. Did she really believe she'd be like Thoreau, escaping to the woods and Walden's Pond to find some inner peace or a deeper meaning to her life? She did know one thing that guaranteed inner peace and was much quicker. A nice bottle of Bordeaux.

She started to turn back toward the cabin when she saw something move down by the lake. She strained to see. It looked like a man moving, sneaking between the trees, almost as if hiding.

Her stomach plunged and her knees went weak. She crouched down so suddenly she crunched leaves and almost lost her flashlight.

Did he hear that? Could he see her? She held her breath and listened. Behind the shrubs she could barely see. She pushed herself up on wobbly knees, just enough to see down by the lake. He wasn't there. Was he hiding? She couldn't see him. Her eyes darted around the shore, up and down the steep edges, between the trees.

The man was gone. He had disappeared as suddenly as he had appeared. She stayed crouching, waiting as though she expected him to appear again. Then she wondered, had there been anyone there at all? Or was it simply her stressed and overactive imagination? They said her grandfather had started to hallucinate before the madness.

She needed to stop this or she really would drive herself mad. He could be a groundskeeper or a hiker or someone simply enjoying an evening stroll around the lake. It was a beautiful evening, after all. Not everyone went mad after dark.

THE CABIN WAS RUSTIC BUT COZY with a fireplace, kitchenette, one small bedroom and modern bath that included a shower. The back door walked out onto an attached screened-in porch that overlooked the treetops and the lake. The moonlight illuminated the cabin through the windows and skylights. The reflection off the lake lit the entire porch.

Shadows of branches danced on the walls and suddenly they looked too much like skeleton arms reaching down for her. Maty flipped on every light switch and every lamp. Then she started to unpack her staples. She needed to get something to eat. Or more importantly, pour something to drink. Settle in. Lock down.

SHE DIDN'T REMEMBER falling asleep.

There was a scream and then a clap of thunder. Maty woke with a jerk, almost knocking herself out of the lounge chair on the porch. At first she didn't know where she was. Her head felt heavy, her vision blurred from too much wine. It took a flicker of lightening to remind her.

But why was it dark? She glanced back inside the cabin. She knew she had left every single light on. She reached for the lamp she had dragged out onto the porch and turned the switch. Nothing. She tried again as another flash of lightening forked across the black sky. The thunder that followed rattled the floor boards. William had warned her about thunderstorms. She hated when he was right.

Another clap of thunder and the rain started, a torrential downpour with no signs of letting up. She liked the sound of rain. There was something comforting about its natural rhythms and the fresh scent of scrubbed wood and dirt.

That's when she remembered the scream. She was sure it was a scream that had awakened her.

Maty tried to get out of the chair, but her head begin to swirl. The wine. She must have drunk the whole bottle. She pushed against the arms of the chair. She tried the lamp switch again. Nothing. The electricity was off. In the dark she fumbled around and found her flashlight. What she really wanted to find was the Advil.

The downpour continued but now the wind pushed it through the screen of the porch. She grabbed her book and blanket before they got soaked. She started to retreat inside, but as she reached for the wine glass she saw a flash of light down by the lake.

Not lightening, or was it?

She gulped what was left in the glass, snapped off her flashlight and sat back down, waiting and staring at the spot where she had seen the flash.

There it was again. It looked like a tunnel of light from a flashlight.

Then she saw him. A man carrying something flung over his shoulder, something that looked large and heavy. He was crazy to be out on a night like tonight.

Maybe the wine really had made her mellow, because his appearance didn't frighten her. Quite frankly she didn't care if someone was stupid enough to be out on a night like tonight.

She was sober enough to realize she was drunk. She actually didn't mind the wet wind coming in on her. It felt good, fresh, and erratic. Her head no longer hurt. Her fingers found the wine bottle. She tipped it, pleased to see a bit left. Poured and sipped and continued to watch.

The man had a long stick and was poking the ground. No, wait, it wasn't a stick. The lightening flickered off the metallic end of a shovel. Wasn't he afraid of being struck by lightening? It certainly wasn't smart digging in the middle of an electrical storm. Maybe it wasn't a shovel at all.

Suddenly tired again, she made her way to the bedroom. On the other side of the lake she thought she saw a light, a lamppost shining bright through the trees. How was that possible? The electricity was out.

Her eyelids couldn't stay open and her head was too heavy to care. She climbed into bed and collapsed into a wonderfully deep, alcohol-induced sleep void of thunder and lightening and strangers digging in the rain.

When Maty woke a second time the digital bedside clock glowed 4:45. The lightning had been reduced to a soft flicker and the thunder, a low rumble in the distance. The full moon broke through the clouds, illuminating the small bedroom.

She reached for the bedside lamp and twisted the on switch. It took her a second to remember that the storm had knocked out the electricity. She looked at the clock again and watched it click to 4:46 and realized it must be battery-operated.

The pain in her head reminded her of the wine. And worse, she had forgotten to take her pills. Out of his sight for less than twenty-four hours and Maty was already breaking her promises to William. But instead of regret or remorse, it felt more like defiance and victory. Silly and childish, but if he insisted on treating her like she was a patient or a child he couldn't blame her for acting like one.

She lay in bed, staring out the window. All she could see from this angle were the shadows of treetops swaying in the breeze. It sounded like the rain had stopped entirely. All was quiet and peaceful, nature's wrath finished for tonight.

Then she heard footsteps.

Maty held her breath and listened. Had she imagined it?

No, there it was again, slow and hesitant – the soft groan of floorboards. Someone else was in the cabin.

She didn't dare sit up. Couldn't move if she wanted to, paralyzed by fear. Her mind reeled. Had she locked all the doors? Yes, as soon as she arrived. But maybe not the porch door when she stumbled to bed.

Oh God, had she left it unlocked?

She strained to hear over the thump-thumping of her heart. Her eyes darted around the room. She had left her backpack and everything in it in the other room.

Minutes felt like hours. She willed herself to stay very still. She kept the sheet pulled up to her chin. Her hands were shaking. She could do this she told herself and tried to focus. She could ease off the bed and roll underneath.

Moonlight filtered in past the tree branches and illuminated the bedroom. Now was not a good time. She wanted to pull the curtains shut. Darkness was the only weapon she had. But she couldn't risk moving. Couldn't risk making a sound. So instead, she kept still. She would pretend to be asleep. Could she do that and not scream? Would it matter?

With the power still out there were no electrical whines of appliance motors turning off and on. She held her breath, straining to listen. She heard a distance train whistle. Leaves rustled in the breeze outside the window. A whippoorwill called from the other side of the lake. No footsteps. No groaning floorboards. Had she imagined it? Was that possible? Oh God, maybe she was going mad.

Maty glanced at the clock and continued to lay still. Ten minutes. Fifteen minutes. It felt like a week. Twenty minutes. No footsteps. The thumping of her heart quieted. The banging in her head grew. Too much wine. Too much stress. And she'd forgotten to take her medication last night. Was that all it was?

She watched the darkness turn to dawn. The night shadows started to fade and disappear from the bedroom walls. When Maty finally convinced herself that her imagination had gotten the best of her, she eased out of bed. Still, she monitored her movement, stopping and waiting, listening. After a few minutes of tip-toeing she felt ridiculous.

She stopped at the bathroom then marched into the kitchenette. She'd brought the staples for breakfast, had loaded the small refrigerator. Even without electricity everything was still cold. Her backpack sat on the counter where she'd left it. She poured herself a glass of orange juice, turned to go out onto the porch. That's when she saw the shadow of a man standing by the door.

Maty gasped and dropped the orange juice, glass shattering.

"You forgot to take your pills last night," William said, walking into the middle of the room where she could see his face.

"You scared the hell out of me. What are you doing here?"

"I reminded you."

It was like he hadn't heard her. He looked tired. His clothes were wrinkled and damp. His shoes muddy.

"How long have you been here? How did you get in?"

"You drank a whole bottle of wine." He held up the empty bottle she had left on the porch. "But you forgot to take your pills."

"William, what are you doing here?"

"I'm not really here," he said this with a grin. "I'm checked in at a conference in Kansas City. I did that yesterday morning. Everyone thinks I'm in my hotel room, behind the do-not-disturb sign, preparing my presentation. My car's in the hotel's parking lot. I rented one to come back?"

"But I don't understand. Why are you here?"

"Because I had a feeling you wouldn't take your damned pills."

"William?"

"I changed them out, you see. A nice little concoction that wouldn't go so well with alcohol. Actually it probably wouldn't go so well with anything, but the alcohol would just be another indication of you going over the edge."

He tossed the bottle aside and that's when Maty noticed he was wearing gloves. And in his other hand he carried a knife, a wide-bladed hunting knife that he held down at his side as if he didn't even realize he had it there.

Panic forced Maty to step backward, slowly away from him until the small of her back pressed into the countertop. Trapped. There was no where for her to go.

"I don't understand," she found herself saying out loud. It only seemed to make William grin more.

"Of course you don't. You've been so self involved in your own stressed out madness that you haven't noticed anything or anyone around you. Where's your pill bottle?"

"But if you haven't been happy – ."

"Where the hell are your pills, Madeline?"

In two steps he grabbed her by the hair and shoved the knife to her throat. His breath was hot in her face, his eyes wide. He smelled of sweat and mud. He looked like a madman.

"It was you. Last night in the woods," she whispered and felt the metal press against each word. "Why?"

This time he laughed.

"I had to make sure you took them, that it looked like you'd gone over the edge. Everyone was supposed to be gone but that boy ranger was still here. He saw me."

"Oh my God. William. What did you do?"

"The son of a bitch would have ruined it all. Then after the storm when I came inside and found you still breathing . . ." He dragged out the last word like it disgusted him.

"You're the one who took the key from the park office door."

"I knew you'd stop at work. It gave me plenty of time to get here."

"You called me from here. The train whistle . . ."

"Make it easier on both of us, Maty. Where are your pills?"

He yanked her head against the cupboard and she thought she might black out.

"Okay," she managed. "Stop, just let me get them."

He let go. Shoved her away and backed up.

Maty rubbed at the back of her head and the tangled knot of hair. She eased herself toward the other end of the counter, hanging on for fear her knees might give out.

She kept an eye on William even as she opened the zipper of her backpack and dug her hand inside. He stayed put, waiting, looking tired, impatient. She hardly recognized this man, his hair tousled and face dirty. He wasn't her husband anymore. No, he was some deranged madman who had killed the park superintendent and was about to kill her.

When Maty pulled the Colt revolver from her backpack William's eyes grew wide. Before he could react, before he could move, Maty shot him twice in the chest. The blasts made her jump each time.

She didn't cry. She didn't scream. Her hands weren't even shaking.

She laid the revolver on the counter. Then she stepped back, opened the refrigerator and poured herself another glass of orange juice. This time she sat down. She wondered if this was what it felt like for her grandfather when the madness took over.

She sipped the juice and said to herself, "Now, where to dump the body."

AUTHOR'S NOTE: *After Dark* was first published in 2010 in the anthology, *First Thrills* edited by Lee Child which included twenty-four other short stories by some of the best thriller writers in the business.

TURN THE PAGE FOR AN EXCERPT

New from ALEX KAVA,
New York Times bestselling author of
Breaking Creed and Silent Creed

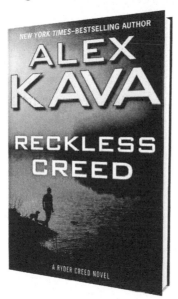

"Original and totally engaging, this new series is
among this reviewer's must-read choices."
~*Phil Jason, Florida Weekly*

RECKLESS
CREED

CHAPTER 1

Chicago

TONY BRIGGS COUGHED UP BLOOD, then wiped his mouth with his shirtsleeve. *This was bad.* Although it was nothing he couldn't handle. He'd been through worse. Lots worse. But still, they didn't tell him he'd get this sick. He was beginning to think the bastards had double-crossed him.

He tapped out, "fine mess I got myself into," on his cell phone and hit SEND before he changed his mind.

The text message wasn't part of his instructions. Not part of the deal. He didn't care. So what if the watchers found out. What could they do to him now? He already felt like crap. They couldn't make him feel much worse.

He tossed the phone into the garbage can along with the few brochures he'd picked up throughout the day. His itinerary read like a sight-seeing family vacation. Or in his case, something presented by one of those make-a-wish charities – one final trip, all expenses paid.

He laughed at that and ended up in a coughing fit. Blood sprayed the flat screen TV and even the wall behind. He didn't like leaving the mess for the hotel housekeeping staff. But it was a little too late for that. Especially since his instructions included touching everything he could throughout the day. The list rattled in his head: light switches, elevator buttons, restaurant menus, remote control, and escalator handrails.

Earlier that morning at the McDonald's – before the cough, just before the fever spiked and he still had a bit of bravado along with an appetite – he felt his first tinge of apprehension. He'd taken his tray and stopped at the condiment counter.

Touch as many surfaces as possible.

That's what he'd been told. Germs could live on a hard surface for up to eighteen hours. He may have screwed up a lot of things in his life but he could still follow instructions.

That's what he'd been thinking when he felt a tap on his elbow.

"Hey, mister, could you please hand me two straws?"

The kid was six, maybe seven with nerdy glasses, the thick black frames way too big for his face. He kept shoving at them, the motion second nature. The kid reminded Tony immediately of his best friend, Jason. They had grown up together since they were six years old. Same schools. Same football team. Joined the Army together. Even came back from Afghanistan, both screwed up in one way or another. Tony was the athlete. Jason was the brains. Smart and pushy even at six. But always following Tony around.

Old four eyes.

"Whadya doing now?" was Jason's favorite catch phrase.

In grade school they went through a period where Jason mimicked everything Tony did. In high school the kid bulked up just so he could be on the football team, right alongside Tony. In the back of his mind he knew Jason probably joined the Army only because Tony wanted to. And look where it got them.

Tony shoved at the guilt. And suddenly at that moment he found himself hoping that Jason never found out what a coward he really was.

"Mister," the kid waited with his hand outstretched.

Tony caught himself reaching for the damned straw dispenser then stopped short, fingertips inches away.

"Get your own damned straws," he told the kid. "You're not crippled."

Then he turned and left without even getting his own straw or napkin. Without touching a single thing on the whole frickin' condiment counter. In fact, he took his tray and walked out, shouldering the door open so he wouldn't have to touch it either. He dumped the tray and food in a nearby trashcan. The kid had unnerved him so much it took him almost an hour to move on.

Now back in his hotel room, sweat trickled down his face. He wiped at his forehead with the same sleeve he'd used on his mouth.

The fever was something he'd expected. The blurred vision was a surprise.

No, it was more than blurred vision. The last hour or so he knew he'd been having hallucinations. He thought he saw one of his old drill sergeants in the lobby of the John Hancock building. But he'd been too nauseated from the observatory to check it out. Still, he remembered to touch every single button before he got out of the elevator. Nauseated and weak-kneed.

And he was embarrassed.

His mind might not be what it once was thanks to what the doctors called traumatic brain injury, but he was proud that he'd kept his body lean and strong when so many of his buddies had come back without limbs. Now the muscle fatigue set in and it actually hurt to breathe.

Just then Tony heard a click in the hotel room. It came from somewhere behind him. It sounded like the door.

The room's entrance had a small alcove for the minibar and coffeemaker. He couldn't see the door without crossing the room.

"Is anybody there?" he asked as he stood up out of the chair.

Was he hallucinating again or had a shadow moved?

Suddenly everything swirled and tipped to the right. He leaned against the room service cart. He'd ordered it just like his watchers had instructed him to do when he got back to his room. Nevermind that he hadn't been able to eat a thing. Even the scent of fresh strawberries made his stomach roil.

No one was there.

Maybe the fever was making him paranoid. It certainly made him feel like he was burning up from the inside. He needed to cool down. Get some fresh air.

Tony opened the patio door and immediately shivered. The small concrete balcony had a cast-iron railing, probably one of the original fixtures that the hotel decided to keep when renovating – something quaint and historic.

The air felt good. Cold against his sweat-drenched body, but good. Made him feel alive. And he smiled at that. Funny how being this sick could make him feel so alive. He'd come close to being killed in Afghanistan several times, knew the exhilaration afterwards.

He stepped out into the night. His head was still three pounds too heavy, but the swirling sensation had eased a bit. And he could breathe finally without hacking up blood.

Listening to the rumble and buzz of the city below he realized if he wanted to, there'd be nothing to this. He had contemplated his own death many times since coming home but never once had he imagined this.

Suddenly he realized it'd be just like stepping out of a C-130.

Only without a parachute.

Nineteen stories made everything look like a miniature world below. Matchbox cars. The kind he and Jason had played with. Fought over. Traded. Shared.

And that's when his second wave of nausea hit him.

Maybe he didn't have to finish this. He didn't even care any more whether they paid him or not. Maybe it wasn't too late to get to an emergency room. They could probably give him something. Then he'd just go home. There were easier ways to make a few bucks.

But as he started to turn around he felt a shove. Not the wind. Strong hands. A shadow. His arms flailed trying to restore his balance.

Another shove.

His fingers grabbed for the railing but his body was already tipping. The metal dug into the small of his back. His vision blurred with streaks of light. His ears filled with the echo of a wind tunnel. The cold air surrounded him.

No second chances. He was already falling.

CHAPTER 2

Conecuh National Forest
Just north of the Alabama/Florida state line

RYDER CREED'S T-SHIRT STUCK TO HIS
BACK. His hiking boots felt like concrete blocks,
caked with red clay. The air grew heavier, wet
and stifling. The scent of pine mixed with the
gamy smell of exertion from both man and dog.
This deep in the woods even the birds were different, the drilling of the red-cockaded wood-
pecker the only sound to interrupt the continuous
buzz of mosquitoes.

He was grateful for the long-sleeved shirt and
the kerchief around his neck as well as the one
around Grace's. The fabric had been soaked in a
special concoction that his business partner, Hannah, had mixed up, guaranteed to repel bugs. Hannah joked that one more ingredient and maybe it'd
even keep them safe from vampires.

In a few hours it would be nighttime in the forest, and deep in the sticks, as they called it, on the
border of Alabama and Florida, there were enough
reasons to drive a man to believe in vampires. The
kudzu climbed and twisted up the trees so thick it
looked like green netting. There were places the
sunlight couldn't squeeze down through the
branches.

Their original path was quickly becoming over-
grown. Thorny vines grabbed at Creed's pantlegs,

and he worried they were ripping into Grace's short legs. He was already second-guessing bringing the Jack Russell terrier instead of one of his bigger dogs, but Grace was the best air scent dog he had in a pack of dozens. And she was scampering along enjoying the adventure, making her way easily through the tall longleaf pines that grew so close Creed had to sidestep in spots.

They had less than an hour until sunset, and yet the federal agent from Atlanta was still questioning Creed.

"You don't think you need more than the one dog?"

Agent Lawrence Tabor had already remarked several times about how small Grace was, and that she was "kind of scrawny." Creed heard him whisper to Sheriff Wylie that he was "pretty sure Labs or German shepherds were the best trackers."

Creed was used to it. He knew that neither he nor his dogs were what most law enforcement officers expected. He'd been training and handling dogs for over seven years. His business, CrimeScents K-9, had a waiting list for his dogs. Yet people expected him to be older, and his dogs to be bigger.

Grace was actually one of his smallest dogs, a scrappy brown-and-white Jack Russell terrier. Creed had discovered her abandoned at the end of his long driveway. When he found her she was skin and bones but sagging where she had recently been nursing puppies. Locals had gotten into the habit of leaving their unwanted dogs at the end of Creed's fifty-acre property. It wasn't the first time he had seen a female dog dumped and punished when the owner was simply too cheap to get her spayed.

Hannah didn't like that people took advantage of Creed's soft heart. But what no one – not even Hannah – understood was that the dogs Creed rescued were some of his best air scent trackers. Skill was only a part of the training. Bonding with the trainer was another. His rescued dogs trusted him unconditionally and were loyal beyond measure. They were eager to learn and anxious to please. And Grace was one of his best.

"Working multiple dogs at the same time can present problems," he finally told the agent. "Competition between the dogs. False alerts. Overlapping grids. Believe me, one dog will be more than sufficient."

Creed kept his tone matter of fact for Grace's sake. Emotion runs down the leash. Dogs could detect their handler's mood, so Creed always tried to keep his temper in check even when guys like Agent Tabor started to piss him off.

He couldn't help wonder why Tabor was here, but he kept it to himself. Creed wasn't law enforcement. He was hired to do a job and had no interest in questioning jurisdiction or getting involved in the pissing contests that local and federal officials often got into.

"I can't think she'd run off this far," Sheriff Wylie said.

He was talking about the young woman they were looking for. The reason they were out here searching. But now Creed realized the sheriff was starting to question his judgment, too, even though the two of them had worked together plenty of times.

Creed ignored both men as best he could and concentrated on Grace. He could hear her breathing getting more rapid. She started to hold her nose higher and he tightened his grip on the leash. She had definitely entered a scent cone but Creed had no idea if it was secondary or primary. All he could smell was the river, but that wasn't what had Grace's attention.

"How long has she been gone?" Creed asked Sheriff Wylie.

"Since the night before last."

Creed had been told that Izzy Donner was nineteen, a recovering drug addict who was getting her life back on track. She had enrolled in college part-time and was even looking forward to a trip to Atlanta she had planned with friends. Creed still wasn't quite sure why her family had panicked. A couple nights out of touch didn't seem out of ordinary for a teenager.

"Tell me again why you think she ran off into the forest. Are you sure she wasn't taken against her will?"

Seemed like a logical reason that a federal agent might be involved if the girl had been taken. The two men exchanged a glance. Creed suspected they were withholding information from him.

"Why would it matter?" Tabor finally asked. "If your dog is any good it should still be able to find her, right?"

"It would matter because there'd be another person's scent."

"We had a tip called in," Wylie admitted but Tabor shot him a look and cut him off from saying anything else.

Before Creed could push for more, Grace started straining at the end of the leash. Her breathing had increased, her nose and whiskers twitched. He knew she was headed for the river.

"Slow down a bit, Grace," he told her.

"Slow down" was something a handler didn't like telling his dog. But sometimes the drive could take over and send a dog barreling through dangerous terrain. He'd heard of working dogs scraping their pads raw, so focused and excited about finding the scent that would reward them.

Grace kept pulling. Creed's long legs were moving fast to keep up. The tangle of vines threatened to trip him while Grace skipped between them, jumping over fallen branches and straining at the end of her leash. He focused on keeping up with her and not letting go.

Only now did Creed notice that Agent Tabor and Sheriff Wylie were trailing farther behind. He didn't glance back but could hear their voices becoming more muffled, interspersed with some curses as they tried to navigate the prickly underbrush.

Finally Grace slowed down. Then she stopped. But the little dog was still frantically sniffing the air. Creed could see and hear the river five feet away. He watched Grace and waited. Then suddenly the dog looked up to find his eyes and stared at him.

This was their signal. Creed knew the dog wasn't trying to determine what direction to go next, nor was she looking to him for instructions. Grace was telling him she had found their target. That she knew exactly where it was but she didn't want to go any closer.

Something was wrong.

"What is it?" Sheriff Wylie asked while he and Tabor approached, trying to catch their breaths and keep a safe distance.

"I think she's in the water," Creed said.

"What do you mean she's in the water?" Tabor asked.

But Wylie understood. "Oh crap."

"Grace, stay," Creed told the dog and dropped the leash.

He knew he didn't need the command. The dog was spooked and it made Creed's stomach start to knot up.

He maneuvered his way over the muddy clay of the riverbank, holding onto tree branches to keep from sliding. He didn't know that Wylie was close behind until he heard the older man's breath catch at the same time that Creed saw the girl's body.

Her eyes stared up as if she were watching the clouds. The girl's Windbreaker was still zipped up and had ballooned out, causing her upper body to float while the rest of her lay on the sandy bottom. This part of the Blackwater River was only about three feet deep. Though tea-colored, the water was clear. And even in the fading sunlight Creed could see that the girl's pockets were weighted down.

"Son of bitch," he heard Wylie say from behind. "Looks like she loaded up her pockets with rocks and walked right into the river."

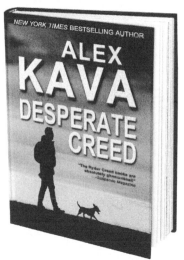
 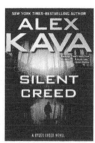 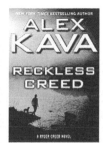 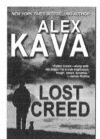

ABOUT ALEX KAVA

ALEX KAVA is the *New York Times* best-selling author of the critically acclaimed Maggie O'Dell series and a new series featuring former Marine, Ryder Creed and his K-9 dogs

Her stand-alone novel, *One False Move*, was chosen for the 2006 One Book One Nebraska and her political thriller, *Whitewash*, was one of *January Magazine's* best thrillers of the year.

Her novel, *Stranded* was awarded both a Florida Book Award and the Nebraska Book Award.

Published in over thirty-two countries, Alex's novels have made the bestseller lists in the UK, Australia, Germany, Japan, Italy and Poland. She is also a co-author of the e-novellas *Slices of Night* and *Storm Season* with Erica Spindler and J.T. Ellison

She is a member of the Nebraska Writers Guild and a founding member of International Thriller Writers.

To learn more about Alex Kava, Maggie O'Dell and Ryder Creed and his K-9 team, follow her on Facebook and become a **V.I.R. member** (Very Important Reader) at www.alexkava.com.

A NOTE FROM THE PUBLISHER

First of all, I want to thank you for reading *OFF THE GRID*. If you have enjoyed it Alex and I would be grateful if you would write a review. It doesn't have to be long—a few words would make a huge difference in *helping readers discover new authors* for the first time.

I also know that Alex would love to hear from you. Please find her on all the social media sites and get in on the conversations on her websites Currently she is working on future books for your enjoyment.

Keep reading!

Deb Carlin

The story of murder, sexual addiction, infidelity, blind devotion and the privilege that comes with power....

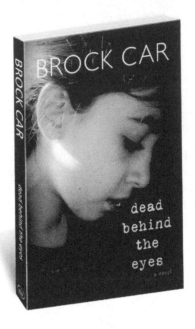

"Ordinary people caught at their worst...
I dare you to guess who did it.."
~*Alex Kava, NY Times Bestselling Author*

Available on Kindle, Nook and trade paperback

Alex Kava believes in rewarding her readers.

Join her
Very Important Reader's Club and

~ be the first to know when the
next book is coming out!

~be auto-eligable to win contests & prizes

~learn cool, interesting behind-the-scenes trivia

~get Alex's annual personalized Christmas card

It's Free to join. Visit:

www.alexkava.com/very-important-readers-club

Follow Alex on Facebook at
www.facebook.com/alexkava.books

Made in the USA
Monee, IL
19 April 2023

32108724R00125